I0554424

The Dancer

Amorous Occupations

Cheryl Barton

Published by:

Barton Publishing, LLC

Barton Publishing, LLC
P.O. Box 962
Reisterstown, Maryland 21136
www.bartonpublishingllc.com

Ordering Information:
Quantity sales. Special discounts are available on quantity purchases by corporations, associations, and others. For details, contact the publisher at the address above.

Orders by U.S. trade bookstores and wholesalers. Please contact publisher@bartonpublishingllc.com

ISBN: 0615918638
ISBN-13: 978-0615918631

ACKNOWLEDGMENTS

Thank you for continuing on with me through this journey of 26 stories of Amorous Occupations. I hope you enjoy reading them as much as I am enjoying writing them. *The Dancer* is book number 4 and I love the instant attraction between Michelle and Kevin. Happy Reading!

"Don't look back because what's ahead of you holds so much promise for a better day and an even better life."
– Cheryl Barton

The Dancer - 1

Max tried to remain calm as the dancer came toward him in the seedy New York night club where he knew no one would recognize him. He was sure his dark attire and the baseball cap sitting low on his head that partially covered his face shielded his identity from anyone who wasn't standing directly in front of him.

He never thought he'd be in a place like this where men came who needed relief from their home lives which consisted of wives and children who placed demands and pressures on them daily. He had neither a wife nor children, but tonight the darkened club with a dozen or so sexy women clambering about trying to entice men and women out of their hard earned money all for a few lap dances, provided the fantasy he needed to do what he came to the club to do.

Max watched several women as they gyrated around the club going from one hand that held out money to the next, hoping to entice a few into something a little more personable. Unbeknownst to them, he wasn't there to get a lap dance. He had other plans in mind for the dancer who was slowly making her way over to him. He'd been trying for several nights to get her attention and had high hopes that tonight would be the night that she'd tune into the signal that he was interested.

As the music played loudly and the liquor poured non-stop, Max sipped on his beer and waited. He didn't have to wait too long once the dancer made eye contact. When he didn't look away, he assumed she thought she had him. Little did she know, she was the one being had.

When she finally reached him, he remained calm, but the rapid tapping of his right foot told another story. He looked at how she was dressed in a hot pink thong, very high heeled clear stilettos and nothing else. He looked at her breasts and could see that she wasn't a very voluptuous woman, but her shape was perfect for him and for how he needed her to look. The familiarity was perfect.

Max let his eyes travel up and down her body as she sashayed around for him making sure he could see her from every angle. When she turned around, showing him her backside, his heart skipped a beat. Now that her face was turned away from him, in his mind he could imagine her looking like anyone he wanted and when the face of the woman he wanted her to be flashed before his eyes, his body jumped with anticipation.

Tonight was finally the night, he thought to himself. He could barely contain his excitement over how the night could turn out. Now that the sexy little vixen was finally about to give him some attention, he knew that his patience had paid off. As she turned back around to face him, coming right up to him he knew it would be the perfect night, at least for him. This time was a long time coming from when he first began his search for the right woman. Max knew she had to be perfect and after not getting the joy and excitement from the first few women he lured in, he had a feeling this one was what he'd been looking for.

Max had come to this place several times, scoping it out. His first visit was to check out the place and to see if any of the women looked like his Shelly. He'd been to several places like this one around the city in hopes that one would resemble the love of his life. An unwavering exhilaration resonated throughout his body the moment he spotted her on his first visit.

The dancer looked so much like his Shelly that they could pass for twins. As the days went by, Max knew that she may be able to pass for Shelly in the looks department, but her dance moves were not up to the standard of Shelly's, who was a professional Broadway actress and dancer. Tonight that fact didn't matter much to him since it wasn't her dancing skills he was interested in.

Steadying his legs as she came up to him became a task as she leaned over so that her naked breasts were mere inches away from his face. Not wanting his nervousness to scare her away, he never took his eyes off of her face, giving her an even, intense stare. It was her face that became the draw and the obsession for him. She had the same beautiful, flawless face as Shelly, though she wore more makeup than he liked. Her long weaved hair flowed down around her shoulders in a cascade of loose curls that he couldn't wait to grasp tightly in his hands. If he thought it wouldn't draw attention to them, he would reach for her now, but he needed to wait. The time for that was getting closer.

"You're watching me," she said in a soft, sultry voice.

Max's body stood at attention.

"Since you came up to me, I assume my watching you intrigued you," he responded.

He was hoping they wouldn't waste a lot of time conversing because he knew it would draw attention from others in the club to them, something he didn't want.

"Well, what will it be tonight handsome?" she asked.

"Not something I can get sitting here."

When she didn't immediately respond, he knew she was thinking about what was obviously a subtle proposition.

"Where would this something you'd like to get need to take place?"

"Well sweetness, it depends on you and what time you get off."

"Well, I'm not really allowed to leave with the customers; it's against club policy."

Max went in for the kill to make sure she changed her mind.

"Well I have a thousand dollars that says your club policy is null and void tonight."

The mention of that much money got her attention when he saw how wide her eyes widened.

"You have a place near here big spender?"

"Not real close by but I have a car that can get us to my place in no time at all and have you back here at the club in time for your stage time in two hours," he replied calmly, not giving away his anxiety.

"How do you know I have stage time in two hours?" she asked.

"I've been coming here for a few nights and you always have the twelve-thirty a.m. time slot for your show. Right now it's only ten and I can guarantee you that I'll have you where you belong by your show time. I'm so riled up for you sugar that I'm sure things will happen quicker than I'd like, but as soon as you need. What do you say to that? Is a thousand incentive enough for you?"

Max knew he was pushing, but if he didn't make

his move tonight, he wasn't sure he'd get another chance. He could see her running the options through her mind, contemplating what she could do with the thousand dollars. He was sure from looking at the clientele, that she'd never make that much money from one customer and in this case, she wouldn't have to split it with the club.

"I could get in trouble and even lose my job if the boss knew I was leaving with a customer, especially one that may spend money in the club tonight."

Max had the answer.

"I'll tell you what I'll do because I really want to spend a little alone time with you. I'll head on out of here, making sure I'm not seen, while you go make an excuse of some type of an emergency, telling your boss you'll be back in a couple of hours just in time for your show. I'm sure you can persuade him to see things your way," Max said, making sure he looked her over from head to toe, letting her know that he meant for her to use her femininity to get her boss to go along with it.

"If I do this, how do I know you actually have this thousand dollars?"

Without any hesitation, Max reached into the inside pocket of his jacket and pulled out a stack of one hundred dollar bills. What he didn't let her see was that only the first five bills were hundreds, while the others were one's, but she was so focused on the hundreds on top and how thick the stack was, that she didn't question him further. He didn't show the money too long, afraid she might catch on so he quickly placed the bills back in his pocket.

"Proof enough for you?" he asked.

"What kind of car do you drive?"

"It's a black Mercedes. I'll pull around the corner so that no one coming in or out of the club will see you get in it. I'll be in it ready to drive off as soon as you get in."

The pull of a thousand dollars for an hour or so with a customer was too big of a pull for her to turn down and Max knew it.

"Give me twenty minutes," she said before turning and walking away.

Max got up, pulled his cap further down on his head to block any view of his face and exited the club. Once outside, he wasted no time getting behind the wheel of the Mercedes he'd stolen a few hours ago from a hospital garage. He'd watched the doctor as he showed up for work, knowing it would be hours, until the doctor's shift ended before he noticed the car was gone. By then, Max wouldn't have a need for it anymore.

Using skills he'd learned as a teenager, he once again connected wires together that started the car up and to add to the illusion for his soon to be passenger, he stuck a fake looking car key in the ignition so that she wouldn't see that he was driving the car without a key. He waited a few minutes and sure enough, he saw her as she exited the club and looked for him. He flashed his lights and waited for her to walk over and get in. Once she got in and buckled the seat belt, he drove off to a spot made just for the two of them and only for tonight.

"Nice car," she said, looking around.

"Thanks. What's your name?" he asked, not really caring.

"It's Candy," she replied.

He knew it wasn't, but again, he didn't care.

"Since I'm paying for this fantasy hour with you, how about I call you Shelly?"

He needed that because it was the only reason she was in the car with him. He needed her to be Shelly for him tonight.

"It's your dime baby, so Shelly it is. What should I call you?" she asked.

"Sugar you can call me Max." He didn't care if she knew his real name. In a few hours, it wouldn't matter.

"Max it is. So Max, what made you pick me? Should I assume it has something to do with a woman named Shelly? Do I resemble her?"

A big talker was something Max couldn't stand. He wanted her to sit in the seat and shut up. He didn't want to scare her by acting strange so he responded.

"That would be a correct assessment. I was in love with a woman named Shelly and you are the spitting image of her."

"Ah ha, hence the fantasy. I understand because strangely enough, I get that a lot from men, especially those at the club. So what are you expecting, something kinky and wild that she wouldn't do for you?"

Max was almost intrigued especially when she said her words as if she were purring like a cat. He decided to play along until he got to the spot where he wanted to be.

"Yeah, something like that. It's just that I miss her like crazy and when I first saw you, I realized if I could get you to agree to some time with me, I could live out a fantasy of a happier time when we were together," he admitted.

"What happened? Did she die or something?"

Max was getting tired of all of her questions.

"No, she left me because I wasn't good enough for her."

"A man with money and a car like this and she thought you weren't good enough for her? She must have been crazy or something."

"Yeah, or something," he replied.

Before long Max pulled up to an area that overlooked the Hudson River where he and Shelly liked to park and sit for hours in his car and enjoy the peace and quiet. When he put the car in park, he noticed a surprised look on his passenger's face.

"Why are we stopped here? I thought we were going to your place?" she asked.

"We are going to my place. I was hoping that for an extra two hundred, you could give me a little attention early, before we got to my place. You're looking so sexy sitting over there in that tight black top and even tighter leopard leggings that I need a little relief now and besides, isn't this a perfect view?" he asked, hoping she'd go along.

Max watched as she looked around to see if there were other people in the area who could see them.

"Don't look so worried. No one is around and the windows are all tinted black. Don't forget, this is a fantasy you're helping me relive and being here in this spot is a big part of that."

To persuade her even more, Max reached into his pocket and pulled off two of the five hundred dollar bills in his pocket and gave them to her.

"Here is the first two hundred and I still have another thousand for you when we get to my place for the real party. Deal?" he asked.

When Candy took the money and put it away in her bag, Max relaxed knowing the night belonged to him.

"See, that wasn't so hard. Now Shelly, how about you slide a little closer while I slide my seat back. I'll need room to unzip and that way you'll have room too."

As he did so, he watched as Candy placed her bag in the area between her seat and the door. As she did so, he moved the seat all the way back and watched her as she watched him unzip his pants for what he had in store for her. He liked that Candy, his Shelly replacement, wasted no time doing what he was paying her to do. He let her work as he leaned back in his seat and thought of Shelly in happier times. He thought about the times when they'd snuggle up in bed watching one of her favorite movies. He thought about all of the times he'd watched her dance in Broadway shows, cheering her on from his front row seat. He imagined her moving gracefully across the stage as if she was floating on air.

As fake Shelly's ministrations became more intense setting his body on fire, he no longer thought of the real passenger in his car, but of the real Shelly that had thrown him away like trash. He thought back to the day that she'd told him they were over and she never wanted to see or hear from him again. He remembered how much he begged and pleaded with her to give him another chance and how much he now hated her for treating him like he was nothing.

The excitement his body would normally feel was replaced by abhorrence and revulsion and in that moment, he remembered why he picked the sexy Shelly look alike. It wasn't to spend a night in her luscious body. It was to take out his revenge until he could satisfy his real lust to watch Shelly suffer for the hurt and pain she'd caused him.

Before he knew what he was doing, Max reached down to his side between his seat and the door, grabbing the pair of gloves he'd placed there earlier. He never opened his eyes because he wanted to keep the image of his Shelly casting him away so that he could do what he'd set out to do. Once he had the gloves on and noticed that fake Shelly never missed a beat as she continued to pleasure him with her mouth, never stopping her action going up and down and increasing the pace, he reached down with both hands, placing them around fake Shelly's neck and squeezed with all of his might. Fake Shelly had no time to scream as she tore at his hands trying to get him to stop as she gasped for air. Max squeezed even harder.

"Die, Shelly. You deserve to die for what you did to me," he shouted. He continued to squeeze and squeeze until fake Shelly was no longer moving. Several minutes after she'd stopped moving he continued to choke her, making sure she was dead.

Max finally removed his hands from around her neck and watched as her head dropped to his lap.

"Serves you right Shelly after all the love and affection I gave you. You were everything to me and you treated me like I was never anything to you. My life is ruined now because of you. Now you'll never treat another man the way you treated me," he said.

Max sat, not knowing how much time had passed before he finally extricated fake Shelly's head from his lap, moving her body completely to the passenger seat. He quickly zipped his pants back up and got out of the car. He looked around to be sure no one was round. He knew there wouldn't be because he and Shelly had come to the spot lots of times and never ran into another person. Taking a few moments to gather his wits, he got out of the car, went around to the other side of the car and opened the door, catching fake Shelly before she had a chance to fall to the ground. He reached in her bag and retrieved the two hundred dollars he'd already given her and then put the bag back where it was. He then went back around to his side of the car, opened the door and unlatched the trunk. He took out the bottle of bleach that he'd purchased earlier at the store and went back to the passenger side of the car. He opened the bottled and began to pour bleach all over fake Shelly, making sure he poured lots of it in her mouth to wash away any traces that a part of his body had been in her mouth. When he was sure she was completely doused, he put the empty bottle in the seat with her, went around to the driver's side once again and this time he released the parking break. Since the car was already facing the water, it didn't take much effort for him to put the car in neutral and push it towards the water. Once he gave it a good running jump start, he slammed the door shut and watched as the car plunged into the water, carrying fake Shelly with it.

The satisfaction Max thought he'd feel didn't happen. He still felt lost, alone and filled with hatred for the woman who crushed his heart and his life. No matter how many fake Shelly's he took his revenge out on, Max knew he would never get real satisfaction until he took his revenge out on the Shelly who'd actually did him in. It was time he put her to rest once and for all. He needed to get home to put his plan in motion.

When the car was finally fully submerged in the water, Max turned and walked away.

"It's your turn now Shelly. There will be no more fake ones."

The Dancer -2

"Shelly, are you being careful in New York?"

"Yes, Pop. I'm being very careful just like you taught me. New York isn't as bad as you think it is and believe it or not, it's not much different than Virginia," Michelle explained to her dad.

A conversation with her father always started off the same way because he worried about her and it made him feel better to hear her say she was fine.

David Hitchens, the man she looked up to as the strongest person she knew was nothing if he wasn't a worrier. She was accustomed to how he was when it came to the safety of his family and she always felt a sense of home when they talked and she heard her father call her Shelly. It was the little, simple things that kept her smiling. If there was anything that she could do to keep him from worrying about her all of the time, she would do it.

She wasn't the only one he worried about. He

was concerned if he couldn't lay eyes on her and all of her siblings at all times. Her mother mentioned the number of times she'd prevented their father from calling to check up on all of them daily. She wasn't their only daughter, but she was their youngest and she was the only one of their children that didn't live in the Virginia area where she was born and raised.

"You know I worry about you being in New York all alone."

"Pop, I'm not alone. Didn't you know there were eight million people living here as well?" she said, trying to add a little humor to the conversation, hoping to ease his concern.

"Unless I've met them all, in my mind, you're in New York all alone, so just watch your back. I know you're out a lot at night by yourself running your dance studio and doing your shows and anything could happen to you. I still wish you would end your classes earlier in the day and not be out so late in the evenings."

Once a cop always a cop, Michelle thought. Her father had been a police chief in the Virginia area and even though he was now retired, the cop in him lived on.

"Pop, please stop worrying. I've been in New York for six years now and nothing has happened so I think you can stop worrying. I've told before, most of my classes are for school aged children that have school all day and a lot of parents depend on after school activities like mine to keep their children occupied and in a safe environment until they get off of work. I'm fine, really I am. How's mom? Is she around?" Michelle asked, trying to change the subject to something a little less serious.

"No, she went with Allie to look at some new furniture. Allie and Donald go to settlement soon on their new home."

Michelle was thrilled for her sister Allison. She gotten married six months ago to a great guy named Donald. Now that Allison was two months pregnant, she and her husband decided to purchase a home and move out of the apartment that would be cramped with the new baby coming.

"Okay, well tell mom I called since I promised her I'd call at least once a week so that you wouldn't have to call me every day," she quipped.

"That's very funny Shelly. You and your mother are always scheming against me," he said jokingly.

"It's not a scheme at all. We're trying to keep you from losing your mind with worry about me. I'll be home in a few weeks to visit. I have a break coming up soon since the studio will be closed for the new remodeling and expansion work that's being done," she said.

"That's good to hear. Your mother will be glad to hear that. I'll let her know that you made your weekly check-in call and be careful."

"I will Pop, I promise," Michelle said before

hanging up.

She loved her father more than anything, but she hated that he spent so much energy worry about her. Neither of her parents were happy when she decided to move to New York to pursue a career in dance. She spent her first few years in New York starring in Broadway and some off-Broadway shows as well. Moving from Virginia to New York was the best decision for her career. She still performed in shows, but her real passion was in the dance classes she taught to children. She loved being able to shape and mold them into wonderful little dancers, teaching them ballet, tap, modern and jazz. Her classes remained full throughout the year and she made a great living as an instructor.

It was due to her success as a Broadway actress and dancer that she was able to finance her dream of owning her own dance studio. She was lucky enough to have the kind of schedule that afforded her the time off three days a week where she could either teach or work with the children to put on small recitals to show their parents what they were learning.

At thirty-one Michelle was pleased with where her life was taking her. She had a flourishing career as a dancer and she was happy that she was able to turn down some opportunities and select only those that fit into her schedule.

It had been her dream to become a dancer since she was a little girl. She remembered her earliest exposure to dance when her family took a trip to New York to see the Christmas play the Nutcracker by the Alvin Ailey Dance Theater. Watching the dancers float around is if they walked on air fascinated her. She pictured herself up on stage mesmerizing the audience with her fluid like moves. When the play was over she wanted more and she wanted to be just like all of the women she'd watched on stage.

On the family trip back to Virginia, her sisters laughed at her when she told them she was going to be a professional dancer just like those women in the play. Her hopes were almost dashed by their teasing until her mother chimed in telling her she could be anything she wanted to be and that if she wanted to be a dancer that she and her father would make sure she was the best dancer she could be. That shut up her sisters and put a smile on her face. She knew if her parents said it then it must be true because they never lied to her.

Once they were back in Virginia, Michelle never forgot about the show in New York and hounded her parents daily about signing her up for dance classes. At the age of six, her father thought she was too young, but her mother saw the gleam in her eyes and knew that she was serious about taking dance. Every day after school she would come home and ask if that was the day they would sign her up. Each day her mother would tell her it wasn't time yet, but she never gave up hope. Then one day when she thought she would get the same response from her mother that she always got, her mother finally said yes. With as much exuberance as she could muster up, she headed straight for the car and waited for her mother to drive her. That first dance class was the best day of her life and from that day, she danced herself into her new career.

She took dance classes and participated in recitals all the way through high school. Her family was elated when she was named dance captain of her high school dance troop and she spent her last two years of high school as the head cheerleader. Combining dance and cheerleading helped her maintain and improve on her dance moves and when she graduated and was accepted into Juilliard School for the dance program, she was over the top happy.

Off to New York she went after high school and she's never looked back. After graduating from Julliard, there were lots of opportunities being thrown at her in New York so she decided to stay and not return to Virginia. Her parents weren't happy, wanting her closer to them, but she assured them she would come home often and that they were only a short drive away from her. Her move to New York after years of school and two additional years of training had been eight years ago and now she was still living her dream.

She knew her family worried about her living in

a big city that was riddled with crime, but so were other cities around the country. She loved New York with all of its bright lights and opportunities for success. As a professional dancer, she couldn't think of a better place to live.

Trying to calm her family's reservations about her living alone in the big city for the first few years was a major task. Every time one of them read a new story of someone being attacked or killed, they would ring her phone, not caring what the hour of the day or night was. Once they heard her voice and found that she was okay, it would quiet them for a little while until the next big news story came out. She wanted and needed them to know that she was taking care of herself and watching her back every day. There were always things happening in New York and her Brooklyn neighborhood was no different. She did like most women did; she carried mace and tried not to be out alone to often late at night.

Since she lived in New York for her entire adult life, she'd developed a nice group of friends and they looked out for each other as much as possible. Of course her mother and sisters asked her when she was going to focus more on a private life and get married and have some babies and less time on her career. Michelle shook her head every time one of them brought it up. They were beginning to sound like a bunch of broken records. She assured them she had plenty of time for marriage and babies and that she did have a dating life that was going very well. She sometimes gave them random stories with random names of guys she knew just to keep them from nagging her.

When she'd actually fallen in love with her ex-boyfriend Max, they were the first she called and told. They couldn't wait to meet him and within six months of her and Max dating, he accompanied her home for the Christmas holiday to meet the family. Her mother and sisters liked him right away, but her dad had reservations. He never told her what his specific issues were with Max, but her dad told her to watch herself and to keep her eyes open when it came to Max. She wasn't sure what he meant back then, but today she did.

Thinking of her relationship with Max which ended very badly, gave her chills as she continued to lay across her bed after ending her phone conversation with her father. Max had eventually turned out to be nothing like the man she thought she'd fallen in love with. Though at one point in their relationship they had enjoyed wonderful times together, it was the not so wonderful times that ended up sticking with her. She'd told her family during her many calls home what a wonderful man Max was and how well he treated her hoping that if she spoke those things they'd be true. In the beginning they were, but as Max began to change, so did the relationship.

All of those things that her family constantly

reminded her to watch out for from strangers in New York were being lived out in her very own relationship. She never told any of them what happened with her relationship with Max. They all accepted without question when she told them it was over and that they'd gone their separate ways. What she didn't tell them was the hell she'd gone through and the terror she'd lived with most days. Now that it was over, she was still trying to move on and that meant wiping all thoughts of Max from her mind as she got ready for her the busy day she had ahead of her. There was lots of work to be done at her studio and she had no time for reminiscing about a relationship gone bad.

The Dancer - 3

"May I speak with Detective Kevin Garner, please?"

"This is Detective Garner," Kevin replied, hoping it was the call he'd been waiting on.

"Detective Garner, this is Phyllis Lockley returning your call about my daughter, Melodi who I reported missing. Your message said you had some additional questions for me?"

Kevin was glad it was the call he was expecting. He didn't have much information to provide to her regarding her missing daughter, but he knew that any additional information she could provide would help in the investigation.

"Yes, Mrs. Lockley, thank you for returning my call. Again, I'm sorry that your daughter is missing and right now I don't have any more information for you. I did have some questions for you and I wanted to see if you could provide some of her medical history or other identifying marks that could help us in finding her."

"Are you saying my daughter may be dead, Detective? I know that the police ask for that type of detailed information when they are looking at a dead body?"

Kevin wasn't trying to upset the mother or insinuate that her daughter was dead. He knew it was a part of his job and he had to start someplace.

"No that's not what I'm saying at all. I have the picture you brought to the police station and that was very helpful, but the more you can provide to us, the faster we can work on locating your daughter. Do you mind if I ask you a few more questions?" he said, trying to move away from any talk of her daughter being dead.

"Okay," she replied.

"Now, when was the last time you actually spoke to your daughter or know of anyone who has spoken to her?"

"Well, she works at a club in a not so good section of the city and I haven't heard from her since Thursday. She told me she was going to work on Friday night and that she'd call me Saturday in the afternoon when she woke up. She works very late at night so I wouldn't hear from her until the next day, usually right around noon after she's worked. She always calls me the next day so that I would know that she was okay. She knows I worry about her working at the club."

"You said she's a dancer there correct?"

Kevin could tell she was hesitating. She didn't have to say it in order for him to know the type of dancer her daughter was.

"Yes she was a dancer and some nights she also did some bartending."

"You didn't hear from her on Saturday and a week later you reported her missing. Why did it take you so long to report her missing?"

"Well, Detective, I like to give my daughter her space and not hover. I thought maybe she'd forgotten to call me and maybe took a quick trip with some friends or perhaps with her boyfriend to Florida. She liked to do that every now and then. My husband always says I'm a worrisome mother and thought that maybe Melodi just needed some space. I knew something was wrong the following Saturday when we didn't hear from her because that was my husband's birthday and she never misses either of our birthdays. That's when I went to the police station to report her missing."

"I understand. I have the boyfriend's name and number and the name and address of the place where she works. Can you give me any other names of friends, co-workers or anyone else that you can think of that Melodi may have had contact with? I want to be sure to cover all bases."

Kevin wrote down the additional names and numbers and before hanging up, he promised her that he'd keep her posted on anything he found out while looking for her daughter.

Kevin stared at the picture of the beautiful young woman and wondered what could have happened to her. He knew that it could have been anything, especially in the city where crime happened as often as one could blink an eye.

The first thing he did after taking down the information on the missing woman was to visit the club where she worked. No one remembered her coming in to work for the week and the last they remembered seeing her, she'd left the bar before her performance over a week ago stating she'd return in time for her set, but never did. None of them found it odd that she never returned because she apparently wasn't the most reliable stripper they'd ever encountered. It was apparent it was something she did often, but they kept her around because she was a big money maker for the club, drawing in the men on a nightly basis.

Kevin had also spoken with Melodi's boyfriend who said that he had been in Las Vegas at a bachelor party the weekend Melodi had gone missing and that he didn't suspect anything was wrong until he returned and hadn't been able to reach her.

Kevin checked into the guy's story and found that he was in Vegas and had been there two days before Melodi disappeared, not returning until the Wednesday after. He claimed they had a great relationship and that he didn't have any problems with her working as a stripper, though Kevin found that hard to believe. What man wanted other men groping on their woman night after night? He sure wouldn't.

He couldn't speak too much about it since he didn't have a woman of his own right now to be groped or to grope himself. Still he continued to check into the guy's story to rule out that he may have had something to do with Melodi's disappearance.

Glancing back down at the picture again before closing the folder, Kevin could tell the twenty-five year old woman was a looker. He also wondered what made women want to work in such an environment where different men palmed them night after night for money. He had a daughter himself and she would never hear the end of it if she even thought about doing something like that. Kevin knew that no matter what Melodi decided to do, she was someone's daughter and she needed to be found.

"Kevin, any leads on that case yet?"

He looked up to see his Captain standing over his shoulder.

"Nothing yet. I've spoken with co-workers, neighbors, family and friends and no one has seen or heard from her since the night she was last at the club. I'm about to make a few more calls to some other contacts I received from her mother, but so far nothing. She has simply vanished like so many other people do in New York City every day."

"Check with the seventy-seventh precinct. I was on the phone with them and I think they have a case similar to this one of a missing stripper and from the description, she could be a twin for your missing person."

Kevin didn't want to think that they were dealing with a serial killer out killing strippers.

"I'll get right on that."

"How's Casey doing?"

Kevin smiled thinking of his daughter who was the light of his world.

"She's fine and hounding me daily about taking dance classes. I'm still trying to work out how I can do that."

"She'd make a pretty little ballerina I'm sure. You know if you need to make some changes to your schedule, you go ahead and do that. Casey needs you just as much as we need you around here, so don't let this job get in the way of doing what you need to do at home. There are enough detectives around here to cover for you."

"I know Captain and I'm working on it. You know how I am about all of these open cases I have and I think I'll be able to work something out with my mother for Casey's classes."

"Great and when she has recitals, let us all know so that we can come out and support her. After having three daughters who all took dance classes, I'm accustomed to sitting through them."

"Will do Captain. I'll let you know if I need to

make any changes."

"Sound good Kevin and let me know what the seventy-seventh has to say about their missing person's case."

Kevin shook his head in acknowledgement as his captain walked away. He appreciated everyone's help around the ninetieth precinct where he worked. Being a single dad was not an easy task and after losing his own wife the way he did, in such a gruesome manner, everyone pitched in and encouraged him as much as they could to help him make it through the day. Casey was his priority, though work was as well. Speaking of Casey, he jumped up when he noticed it was time for her to get out of school and he'd promised her he'd pick her up. He grabbed the case folder and sprinted for the door.

The Dancer - 4

"Good morning, this is Michelle Hitchens and I'm calling about the costumes for the dance production taking place at your theater tomorrow evening. I want to be sure they all arrived today," she said when someone finally answered the phone.

Michelle had been calling most of the morning and couldn't get an answer. She was planning to head over to the theater around lunchtime, but she wanted to be sure the costumes had arrived. If they had not, she would need to get on the phone with the designer immediately to see what the hold-up was.

"Oh yes, they're here, Ms. Hitchens. We've been busy all morning getting the final pieces to your set together and I personally checked the costume order to be sure everything was included according to the instructions you left with us last week. Will you still be coming to take a look at everything today?"

Michelle was relieved.

"Yes. I'll be there around noon. Is that a good time?" she asked.

"That's a perfect time. We'll have everything completed by then."

"Great," Michelle replied. "Thank you for all the work you've done to help me get this production ready on time."

"We are glad to help and are always willing to help when it comes to seeing the smile on a child's face and watching them perform, showing their talents, especially those doing it for the first time. I think you'll be pleased with everything. We'll see you around noon," the woman said before disconnecting the line.

Michelle was excited because everything was falling right into place. Her assistant would be meeting her at the theater at noon and they would make sure everything was ready for the performance the next night.

She enjoyed watching all of the hard work the children put into each class come together for a great production. They have been working for months on the recital and she was just as excited as the children were. Finally being able to showcase their hard work to all of their families and friends was what the recital was all about.

Several of her friends were coming out to support the recital as well. They were a great support system for her since all of her family was in Virginia. They not only support her studio and its many performances, but they also came out to her Broadway performances too. She appreciated their support and knew that they were being more supportive than ever since her breakup with Max.

At one time, they hung out together, including Max, but towards the end of her relationship, her friends started distancing themselves. They noticed a change in Max before she paid any attention to it. They stayed in contact with her, but would decline invites she extended if they knew the invite included Max's presence.

It wasn't until one of her best friends opened her eyes to the abuse she was suffering through in her own relationship that Michelle realized she was suffering the same with Max.

Her relationship with him started out good and one day, without any sign that something was wrong, things turned pretty bad. He became a jealous boyfriend and would often follow her and question her in the presence of others if he saw her talking to another man. His behavior shocked her and those around her.

For almost a year things were wonderful and then one day he snapped and became accusatory. In his mind she was seeing other men and playing him for a fool. He even accused her of sleeping with the husbands of some of her friends, something she blatantly denied. What triggered his jealous rage, she didn't know. All she knew was he wasn't the Max she'd fallen in love with.

They'd met when she was the lead dancer in a major Broadway production and he was one of the executive producers of the show. Once things started breaking down for him, he'd lost his job and had a hard time getting another one because he was such a loose cannon. When she finally saw the change in him, she initially tried to help him. She offered to go to counseling with him, which made him more aggressive. What finally made her leave was the one and only time he'd hit her. It wasn't a hit hard enough to leave a mark of any kind, but the thought that he'd struck her woke her up and she knew that he was beyond help. Offering to help him if he was willing to seek the help wasn't going to work and he wasn't open to it.

The day that he'd struck her she realized he didn't even flinch at the thought that he'd actually struck her. He was enraged and after the physical assault, he issued threat after threat of more harm if she didn't do everything he told her to do and do it the way he wanted.

Max never wanted her to talk to another man, not even in a professional sense. He told her if he saw any interaction with men, she would regret it. Frightened at the thought of him following through on his threats, that same day after he'd left her house, she had the locks changed and had an alarm company come out to install a secure alarm system.

She stayed with friends to regroup and before going back home, she went to see him at a friend's house where he'd been staying and with her friends in tow, told him that they could no longer be involved because she now feared him and he needed to get some help. When she'd asked that he not contact her anymore, he showed no emotion and it frightened her. Max looked at her and her friends with an eerie blankness and without saying anything, he walked away and she'd never heard from him again. That had been a year ago and her life had finally gotten back to normal. She didn't know what finally became of Max and no one else in the dance world knew what became of him either. Images of him ever being a part of her life had slipped into non-existence.

Michelle wiped thoughts of that bad time in her life out of her mind and replaced it with happier thoughts of the recital and all of the children who made her life a joy every single day.

**

Max woke and turned on the television to watch the morning news. So far there had been no reports on any bodies being found in the Hudson River. After dumping the car with the stripper in it over a week ago, nothing had surfaced including any news on any others he knew he'd dumped as well.

He still waited for the satisfaction to settle in that he had taken his revenge for the way Shelly had treated him. He wasn't trash, though she'd thrown him out of her life like he was and he didn't appreciate it.

Now that he knew no one had discovered his secret burial place, it was time to seek his ultimate revenge by no longer hunting down fake Shelly's. It was time he made the real Shelly pay for what she'd done.

It was because of her that he was living on skid row. His career was over and all of his friends had alienated him, saying he'd changed and not for the better. It was all her fault. They could have had a wonderful life together if she hadn't been a liar and a cheat. Though she never admitted that she slept around, he knew she often did when he wasn't around watching her day and night, something he had to resort to in order to keep her in check.

Shelly was a beautiful woman, more gorgeous than any woman he'd ever met. There wasn't a man around who could resist her and he spent all of his time making sure none got close enough to her to make her want to leave him. The fact that she broke up with him made him see that she had been seeing someone all along. He couldn't think of another reason she would break off their relationship.

For months now he'd been watching her and knew that she was being really slick about the man she must be seeing. She must know that he's watching her, so she doesn't flaunt her new lover in public yet, but he was waiting for the day when she did knowing it would be the guy's last day on earth too.

Just the thought that she may have a new lover had him seething with hatred. He didn't want another man touching her or making love to her. That right was reserved only for him. He'd make sure the new guy, whoever he was, would end up sleeping eternally at the bottom of the Hudson along with her. Max knew deep down that he didn't really want to hurt Shelly, but she'd made it very clear she wanted nothing to do with him so he needed to make sure no one else would have her either. He just needed to put his final plan in place. He knew that soon she'd have a vulnerable time and then he'd make his move.

"Hey buddy, you have until tomorrow to pay this week's rent on the room."

Max jumped at the pounding on his door. He ignored it as usual and would get him his rent money when he felt like it. The room wasn't even worth the thirty dollars a week Max paid to live there. It was dirty, noisy and roach infested. What he hated most was the blinking red motel sign that flashed through is window at night, making it hard for him to get any sleep. The bed made a loud squeaky noise every time he moved around on it and he hated to think of who slept on the sheets that were supposed to be white, but were instead a dingy yellow. The little bathroom wasn't worth showering in. He would probably get a disease just from using the tub that had a brown ring around it that bleach couldn't even get out. He was a long way from the beautiful home he'd lived in with Michelle, his Shelly.

"I'll have your money," he yelled back through the door.

"You better or you are out of here buddy."

Max didn't care because soon he wasn't planning on coming back anyway. If he played his cards right, he would put Shelly to sleep soon and he would take off for the west coast leaving her and the miserable way his life turned out because of her behind him for good. For now, nothing was said on the local news about bodies being found so putting his plan in place to add one or maybe two more bodies to his count wouldn't get noticed either. He hoped that was the case at least until he was far away from New York.

**

"Dad, you promised we could go to the recital. You promised!" Casey exclaimed to her father when he tried to make an excuse for why they wouldn't be able to go.

"Casey, I know I said that we could go, but something has come up at work. We'll go to the next recital, okay? I promise," Kevin said to his very disappointed seven year old daughter.

"You always say you promise and you don't keep your promises," she said, crossing her arms across her chest and flopping down on the sofa.

Kevin didn't like disappointing his daughter. He

also hated that his work as a detective for the New York Police Department sometimes took him away from her at times when they'd made plans. Today it couldn't be helped. Not only did he have a missing person's case on his hands, but someone had been randomly attacking women around the city and he was one of the detectives responsible for solving those crimes as well. Something about the attacks made him think that they may be connected to the three missing strippers, one in his precinct and two others in another precinct. A lead had come in that he needed to follow-up on and that would involve them missing the recital.

Looking at his little girl, his heart broke that he had to once again disappoint her and go back on a promise he made to her.

To console her, he went over and knelt down in front of her just as tears began streaming down her face.

"Casey I'm sorry sweetie and you know daddy wouldn't cancel out on you for anything if this wasn't important."

"Everything is always important except for me," she grumbled.

"Now Casey, you know that's not true. You are the most important person in my life and nothing and no one means more to me than you."

"If that was true then you would forget about your work and we could go to the dance recital. Please daddy?" she pleaded with eyes that would melt the coldest heart.

It wasn't a cold heart Kevin was dealing with. It was his job and he had to get whoever is attacking and assaulting women around the city off of the streets and if possible find a connection to his missing person. He had been given a good solid lead on a suspect and he needed to do his job.

"Daddy is very sorry Casey and I promise, promise, promise I'll make this up to you. We'll do something Sunday okay?"

These are times when he hated his job the most. He didn't like having to put anything ahead of his time with her.

Kevin knew Casey loved him very much, even when he disappointed her. They had each other and though sometimes he had to change plans they may have made, he made a point of showering her with attention with every bit of free time he had.

The one sacrifice he knew he made was to his personal life of which he had none. He didn't make much time for dating because of how hectic his work schedule was and when he did have time away from work, he made a point of giving all of that time to Casey.

"I'll tell you what, why don't you pick a show for us to see Sunday and I'll get us some tickets while I'm at work today. Would you like that?" he said.

He knew that would do the trick. Casey loved going into the city to see a play. He watched as several emotions played across his daughter's face before she finally uncrossed her arms and smiled at him.

He decided to take it up another notch.

"You can even pick where you want to eat after the show and I'll even dress up," he said.

"Can I wear my blue dress?" Casey said with enthusiasm.

The life was coming back into the conversation and Kevin was happy.

"You sure can. Why don't you go and make sure it's clean while I finish packing your lunch for school," he said.

He stood as Casey hopped up happily off of the sofa and headed to the stairs. She had just about reached them when she turned back around and ran back to give him a hug.

"I love you daddy and I'm sorry I was so mad at you."

"I love you too pumpkin and daddy understands. I don't like breaking promises to you and we'll have lots of fun Sunday, okay?" he said.

He watched as Casey shook her head yes and then ran once again for the stairs to check for her blue dress.

Another crisis averted Kevin thought as he went into the kitchen to finish packing Casey's lunch for the day. It was Friday and he knew it was a peanut butter and jelly sandwich kind of day. It was the one thing for lunch that Casey loved to have and they agreed that she could take one every Friday.

It wasn't an easy job raising a seven year old by himself, but he felt like he was doing a pretty good job, despite the loss of her mother. Thoughts of Casey's mother entered his mind as he continued making her lunch.

He and Casey's mother, Sharon, had been married for a year when Casey had been born. Sharon loved being a mother, but she began to abhor being the wife of a police detective. His job took him away from Sharon and Casey often and three years into their marriage Sharon began engaging in an affair with another man. Things had become serious between them, unbeknownst to Sharon, who thought she and the man were having some fun on the side. When she tried to back out of the affair, the man she'd had the affair with killed her by smothering her with a pillow and while he straddled her body with the pillow over her face, he stabbed her over and over again to prevent her from leaving him. They'd snuck off to a hotel that day for some afternoon fun and when Sharon told him she wouldn't leave her husband and daughter for him, her lover killed her in a fit of rage and left her body lying like a broken rag doll in the hotel bed naked.

Kevin remembered that day as if it had just happened, even though it had been a few years. He was at work when his boss called him in the office to break the news to him. They'd gotten the call that it was Sharon and he wanted to be the one to tell him. Even though they tried to keep him from going to the hotel to see if it was true, he did go and wished every day after that he had not. He has never been able to get the image of his wife laying across the bed with over twenty stab wounds in her chest. The most gruesome part of the scene was the fact that the knife was still embedded in her chest when he got there as they waited for her body to be removed by the medical examiner and taken for an autopsy. The investigation would later reveal the affair and lead them to the man who had taken Sharon's life. When they were able to get the warrant for his arrest, he'd killed himself before he could be arrested.

Kevin had blamed himself for a long time after Sharon's death. If it wasn't for Casey, he wasn't sure he would have been able to put his life back together. He didn't know Sharon was unhappy to the point that she'd turned to another man for fulfillment. Now it was just he and Casey and as much as he knew he had a job to do, when he wasn't working, all of his time was spent with her because he never wanted her to feel like she didn't have a parent at all.

Kevin was also thankful for his mother. She helped him out with Casey especially since his schedule was often hectic and she was available to help him when it came to Casey's care. After school, the school bus would take Casey to his mother's house and she'd keep Casey until he would come to pick her up and take her home. She didn't live far from them and for those times when he had emergencies at work, he would pick his mother up and she'd come over to look after Casey for him.

He often wished he could carve out more time for Casey to have more after school activities. His mother didn't drive and that made it hard for them to plan anything extra for Casey to do. He was against his mother and Casey taking the subway, so until he could work out a better work schedule, Casey would have to be patient with him. For now, he was glad that she understood his having to cancel out on the dance recital. He needed to consider some type of change. Casey needed more activities besides hanging with him all of the time. Somehow he'd work something out and hopefully he'd be in a better position to do so once this case was solved.

The Dancer - 5

"Michelle let's go grab a bite to eat."

Michelle was a bag of nerves. The dance recital was one day away and she was excited and nervous at the same time. Right now her best friend, Lila was trying to get her to relax.

"Lila, I'm too worked up to eat. The kids have worked so hard for this recital and I'm excited for them. I just hope everything goes off without a hitch tomorrow," she said.

"Everything will be fine, now grab your coat and let's go. There is no need for you to sit here all evening since you closed the studio tonight to give the kids a night of rest and relaxation. You should do the same. I'm starving and I know you are too, so let's go eat girl!" Lila exclaimed.

Michelle knew her friend was right. She needed to get her mind off of every little detail about the recital, trying to find something she forgot to do and just relax.

"Okay and I'll drive since my car is in the garage so you won't have to move yours," Michelle offered.

Lila lived a few houses down from Michelle and parking was a nightmare on the street where they lived. Luckily Michelle had a garage attached to her brownstone so parking wasn't a major issue.

Michelle was thankful for their friendship. Lila was a very successful make-up artist and they had become good friends not long after Michelle had moved to New York.

"That sounds good to me and I never miss an opportunity to not move my car," Lila admitted.

Michelle grabbed her things and they walked to her adjourning garage.

"I'm driving so you pick a place to eat."

"Let's go to anything Italian since I love Italian food and more than that, I love looking at Italian men."

Michelle laughed at her man crazy best friend.

"You and men. I'm surprised you aren't out with one tonight."

"I could have been, but I knew you were going to be a wreck tonight so I thought I'd help relax you before your big night tomorrow."

"You are right about that because my nerves are on overdrive. Thanks for volunteering to do the make-up for everyone."

"No thanks needed," Lila said. "You know I would do anything for you and those kids. I love them like they're all my own. All fifty of them," Lila said laughing.

"Hey it wouldn't hurt you to check out an Italian man or two yourself. You are way overdue for some attention from the male species."

"Lila, don't start with me. I'm still not ready yet. Besides, I have been extremely busy with the studio and I don't have time for men right now. Soon the studio will be closed for a few weeks for the remodel and expansion and while that's happening, I'll be working on getting the word out about the new classes. I'm adding on four new classes during the week and three new instructors. As you can see, I have a lot going on, not to mention I agreed to do a few shows myself."

"How long are you going to sing that same old song? You are more than ready and you're always busy, so that's no excuse. You have time for the studio and men. You're just scared and you need to let go of the past. What happened to you with Max is not what would happen with every man you meet. It's time for you to get back out there and you know you would have the time if you really wanted to."

Lila was right, she thought to herself. As she drove to the restaurant brief thoughts of Max again entered her mind and she quickly dismissed them. She knew all men were not like him. She would love to be in a relationship with a wonderful man like the one's her two sisters had married. Right now it wasn't in the cards for her. She just hoped that one day when her card was played, she'd find her prince and not the frog.

"I know Lila. Just give me a little more time. I can't be jumping the bones of every man who shows interest in me since I'm not you," she quipped, while giving her friend the side eye.

"Hey you do you and I'll continue to do every Italian man in New York. A sister has needs girl and unlike you, I don't believe there are enough batteries in the State of New York to ever help satisfy this beast," Lila said, making mention of her over the top sexual appetite.

"Whatever girl," Michelle said, shaking her head at her friend. She appreciated Lila because only she could take her mind off of the recital and have her laughing over New York's lack of supply of batteries.

Michelle picked one of their favorite places to eat and as soon as they were sitting in front of big plates of spaghetti and lasagna, all thoughts of being nervous about the recital dissipated.

"Oh my goodness, I have no business eating this heavy pasta. I'm going to gain twenty pounds after this," Michelle said.

"Girl stop with that foolish talk. You never, ever gain an ounce and all I ever do is see you shove food in your mouth. Just eat and enjoy it. You don't hear me complaining and I'm not as active as you are."

"Lila, you look fine and I don't see any extra weight on you either and I know how much you love to eat, especially this fattening Italian food."

"Don't look now, but I think there are some guys checking us out."

Michelle didn't even attempt to look. She had no interest in anyone at the moment and she wasn't trying to pick any up.

"You can't even enjoy a nice dinner without your radar tracking down every man who smiles our way. What is it with you? You don't have enough men already?"

"Please, I'm only thinking about you. My sex card is completely full for the month, but you on the other hand could use a little pick me up in that department."

"I do not need a sex pick me up, Lila, so stop it," Michelle said laughing.

"Girl, I bet the last time you got some was from that tired ass Max, and yes I said tired ass. Don't forget you told me the sex with him was lazy because you were bored with it. What was it that you told me? Oh yeah, you said that it had become as exciting as watching paint dry. Those were your words not mine."

Michelle almost choked on her spaghetti.

"You are lying through your teeth. I never told you anything like that."

"Sure you did and I remember the conversation very clearly. I was telling you about the marathon sex I'd had with Mario, the Italian stallion from my gym and when I was done, you said you were jealous because the sex you'd been having lately with Max was like watching paint dry."

Michelle knew it was true, she just didn't want to admit it. There was a time early in the relationship when making love with Max had been wonderful. He wasn't her first experience, but at the time, he had been her best until things between them had gotten bad. They went from making love to having sex for the sake of having sex. She did it because she felt obligated, but she no longer felt emotionally vested with him. He began to use sex as more of a means to have control over her and not because they had a loving connection. There was no longer any caressing, cuddling or any type of foreplay. He would strip her clothes off and mount her like an animal in heat and his sweet, soft words of love during love making had turned into harsh, abrasive demanding words, wanting her to tell him he was the best she'd ever had and that she belong only to him. Lila was right in her recollection of what she'd told her. It had turned into a chore and no longer held any enjoyment for her.

"Yeah, well, that's in the past."

"Are you saying you've getting some lately?" Lila asked.

Michelle knew that wasn't true and she never lied to her friend even to save face.

"No, I'm not and you're right that I haven't had

any since Max."

"Girl, that stuff is going to dry up. It's been almost a year since you ended your relationship with Max. You must have a lot of stock in battery companies," Lila laughed.

"I'm just not ready and I don't want a parade of bed partners. In the beginning of my relationship with Max, things were great and that's the kind of relationship I long for, not the end, but all of the stuff that came before that. I don't know what caused Max to change as he had, though I suspect he was probably bipolar and had never been diagnosed or treated. Something made him snap and he never snapped back, nor would he seek any help. My relationship with him may make me hesitant at the moment, but it hasn't soured me on having a long lasting, loving relationship. I'll leave the parade of sex partners up to you and live vicariously through you for now."

"Well one of those guys watching us is definitely biting and you know I have no problem being the aggressive one. I'll be right back."

Before she could object to Lila's getting up and picking up the guy, she was already gone from the table and when she turned her head to look at her, she was already happily engaged in conversation where they were both smiling and already getting snuggly. Michelle wished she could be that brazen, but she didn't want to give men the wrong idea about her. She enjoyed sex as much as the next woman, but she wanted it from a man that she could see something long-term happening with; not a one night stand, which Lila was the queen of.

**

"Casey, do you want to watch a movie tonight?"

"No grandma."

Even though she was happy that she and her daddy would be spending Sunday together at a show and then dinner and she'd get to wear her favorite blue dress, she was still sad that she would miss Alyssa's dance recital.

Alyssa was one of her best friends at school and she had invited Casey and her dad to her Saturday dance recital, but because he had to work, she couldn't go.

Most of her friends from school were taking dance classes at the Feet-fantastic Dance Studio. Casey wanted to take classed too, but she knew that she couldn't because of her daddy's work. She tried not to be too sad about it because her grandma told her that he was doing the best he could since her mother had died. She wanted to be with her friends and couldn't. She loved her grandma too and she knew that she had the best grandma in the world. She was too sad to watch a movie and she wanted to go to the recital.

"I picked up some cookie dough yesterday and we could make a big batch of cookies. What about that?" her grandma asked trying to come up with things to do that would take away some of the sadness.

"No thanks grandma. I'm just going to watch Nickelodeon," she said, sadly.

"Casey you know your dad is very sorry about the recital tonight. This is a very important case he's working on. I told you how someone has been hurting women all over the city and your daddy is trying to stop him from hurting anyone else."

"I know grandma."

Charlotte didn't know what else to say or do to bring a smile to her granddaughter's face. She was about to suggest another idea when her front door opened and in walked Kevin. They both looked up in surprise since he was supposed to be at work all night.

"Where's my pumpkin," he said.

"Here I am daddy."

Casey jumped up from the sofa to leap in his arms

"What are you doing here, daddy? Aren't you still working?"

"Not anymore tonight I'm not because I'm taking my favorite girls to a recital tonight.

"We're going to the recital?"

"We sure are. I was telling some of the guys at work about how sad you were about missing the recital and they agreed to do my work for me tonight so that I could spend some time with you. How does that sound?" he asked, knowing the answer.

He got his answer right away by the tight grip Casey had on his neck, hugging him tight.

"Thank you daddy," she said.

"Anything for you, pumpkin. Now why don't you and grandma go get ready for the recital because we have just enough time to get there and get good seats before it starts?"

Casey jumped right down out of his arms and grabbed her grandmother's hand.

"Come on grandma we have to get dressed. Daddy's taking us out."

He smiled watching them hurry about.

After waiting for less than a half-hour, they were all dressed up and ready to go.

They arrived at the theater with plenty of time to spare.

"Here, these are good seats, daddy," Casey said finding three seats on the second row.

"These sure are," Kevin said taking his seat after Casey and his mother were seated.

When every seat in the theater had been filled, the lights dimmed signally the start of the show.

He looked up just in time to see a beautiful woman walk out on the stage. To him, she walked with a grace that made her look as if she were gliding across the stage. She was dressed in dance attire, a leotard, tights and a dancer's skirt. He was awestruck from the moment the first words came from her mouth. Though he was listening as she spoke, he didn't comprehend much because he was too busy staring at her. Her hair was pulled tightly into a bun at the nape of her neck. Her legs were toned and shapely and they went along well with her very slim, but shapely body.

Kevin's body felt warmer than usual, as if someone had turned off the air in the theater. He look around quickly and didn't see anyone having a reaction as if they were warm so he figured it must be him. He was having an unusual yet immediate reaction to the lovely woman on the stage. As she continued to speak, welcoming everyone to the production, one word escaped through his lips before he knew what he was saying,

"Beautiful," he said, to no one.

"Did you say something Daddy?"

Kevin didn't realize someone could have heard his one word utterance.

"No," he quickly replied. 'Focus Kevin,' he said to himself.

For the rest of the show, which he actually enjoyed a great deal, it didn't escape him that every time the woman, he now knew to be the dance instructor and owner of the studio putting on the performance, came on to the stage, his attention was drawn to her. He found himself searching for her on the stage, even off to the side while the children were performing. He watched as she stood off to the side like the proud momma watching over her flock, showing excitement with every move they made. Every time he saw her smile, he would smile as if she was smiling directly at him.

At the end of the night, everyone gave the recital a standing ovation. Kevin had to admit that the children had done a remarkable job. They looked like they were having a lot of fun and he could tell they'd put in a lot of hard work. Now he knew why Casey was interested in taking dance; each child looked like they were having the time of their life. He could see his daughter dancing around like a princess and grinning from ear to ear. He had to find a way to make it happen for her.

As he stood off to the side with his mother, he watched as Casey ran off to say hello to several of her friends who were in the recital and those who attended as guests.

"This was really nice, son. I'm glad you were able to work it out so that you could take Casey to the recital. I didn't know what else to do to make her smile before you showed up. I even thought about offering her money," his mother said, laughing.

"Mom, I know that I have to try to do better in balancing work and my time with her. I know that my team at the precinct will help out more with my cases so that I can spend time with Casey. Being the lead detective in my unit makes me feel more responsible for being there and being dependable. I just have to learn to take them up on their offer to fill in for me so that I can give her more of my time. She's growing up so fast and now comes the time when she wants to do more things like dance and field trips. I appreciate all you do, but I also have to step things up more."

"That's good and as you can see, the trip to the recital tonight really made Casey's day. Are you still taking her to the show Sunday as well?"

"Of course that's still on. Are you sure you don't want to go? I still have time to get a ticket for you too," Kevin offered.

"No, you and Casey need this quality time together. Tonight was enough for me. Sadie from my church has invited me and some other ladies so I'll be busy. You two have fun together," she said.

"Daddy, I'm hungry," Casey said, walking up and joining their conversation.

"Okay, let's go eat then. There is a really nice place not far from here that we can walk to for pizza."

As they walked toward the exit, he tried to get one last look at the dance instructor, whose name he remembered was Michelle. He would have liked to have had the chance to talk to her to find out a little more about her, but he knew tonight wasn't the night for that. Perhaps he'd see her again or maybe he'd make an impromptu stop at her studio one day since he also had that information thanks to the programs that were given out at the start of the show.

Kevin's thoughts stayed on Michelle all the way to the pizza shop where he ordered a large pizza with everything like he and Casey liked.

"This pizza is good daddy. Have you eaten here before?" Casey asked, while shoving yet another piece of pizza in her mouth.

"Yes, I come here sometimes on my breaks when I'm working. It's usually crowded during the day, but I see there aren't many people here tonight."

He was about to eat another slice himself when he looked up just in time to see the dance instructor from the recital enter. She was alone and no longer wearing her dance attire. She was now in a beautiful royal blue wrap dress that hugged her statuesque body in a way that flattered her and didn't make her look cheap. He looked down and noticed that her feet were encased in high heeled shoes that matched her dress and those long toned legs looked even better than they had earlier. Again, he couldn't take his eyes off of her. It wasn't until his daughter spoke again that Kevin realized he was as still as a statue and was staring at the gorgeous sight in front of him.

"Daddy, that's the lady from the recital. I think she's the teacher or something like that. Alyssa told me when I went to say hello. I'm going to go say hello," Casey said before jumping up from her seat.

"Careful Casey and slow down," Kevin said getting up to follow his rambunctious seven year old.

"Hi, my name is Casey. I loved your recital a lot. My daddy won't let me take dance lessons yet, but we go to see a lot of shows with a lot of dancing and

I like it," she rambled on.

Kevin wasn't shocked at how friendly Casey was. He was glad that she was only like this when he was around. He'd taught her a lot about talking to strangers without him around and he knew she followed his instructions well.

"Well hello Casey. My name is Ms. Michelle and I'm glad you enjoyed the recital. Did you know anyone who participated in it?"

"My friend Alyssa dances with you and she invited me. I know some of the other children too from school," she said happily.

"Alyssa is one of my best students. I will be sure and tell her that I met you tonight," Michelle said before looking up from Casey and staring into the deepest, darkest, sexiest eyes she'd ever seen on a man. His handsomeness started with his eyes and spread out from there all over his face. His good looks practically stole her breath away.

Time seemed as if it stood still as her gaze never wandered away from him. His skin color was the rich color of chocolate mocha and he was built with the body of her favorite actor, Vin Diesel. As she stared from his face then taking a quick stroll down his body he was definitely just as sexy. As her eyes passed back up to his face, her heart fluttered when he smiled at her showing a perfect set of white teeth.

Michelle was having a moment like none she'd ever experienced before. Her mind went quickly back to the night she and Lila were having dinner and talking about how a man was missing from her life and suddenly realization flashed before her eyes when she'd lain eyes on the hunk before her. Her body recognized the close proximity as well because the most private, intimate and sensitive parts of her reacted with pleasure to what her eyes were seeing. Before she could gather herself to greet him, Casey interrupted the moment.

"Daddy, aren't you going to say hello to Ms. Michelle?"

Of course he was. He just needed to find his tongue and get his mind to coordinate with it.

"Hello, I'm Casey's dad, Kevin Garner. It's nice to meet you," he said extending his hand.

"It's a pleasure to meet you Mr. Garner, I'm Michelle Hitchens," she said.

"Just Kevin," he said in response.

"Okay, then it's a pleasure to meet you Kevin and you have a beautiful daughter."

"Thank you and I apologize if Casey interrupted you. She saw you from the table and remembered you from the recital."

"It was no interruption at all. I'm glad she came over."

Michelle looked to see that another woman was sitting at the table where Kevin and Casey had come from. She waved at her so that she didn't forget to acknowledge her as well.

"That's my mom who was also at the recital. We

really did enjoy it."

"I'm glad. The kids worked really, really hard on it. Perhaps I'll see you at another recital."

"Perhaps you may. Well we'll let you get back to ordering your food. It was really nice to meet you," Kevin said before taking Casey by the hand and heading back to his table.

"Bye Ms. Michelle," Casey hollered behind her.

"Bye Casey," Kevin heard Michelle say before turning back around to complete her order.

Kevin's heart didn't stop beating fast until Michelle had received her food and had exited. He couldn't seem to look away. He wished he had taken the time to perhaps ask her out for coffee or something sometime. He wasn't sure how to handle it with Casey standing right there, so he missed his opportunity. He was sure there would be another one.

The Dancer - 6

Max was watching her and she didn't even know it. He was jumpy and excited that he was about to get the chance to be up close and personal again with the love of his life. She was the one woman who had taken his love and stomped all over it like it meant nothing to her. He could barely contain himself knowing that he would soon have his hands on her once again, but the difference tonight would be him using them to snuff the life right out of her, as she had done when she'd left him. She was poison as far as he was concerned and she needed to be dealt with.

He stood across the street in the shadows of the dark buildings where he was hidden from view. He'd followed her all the way from the theater where he knew she'd had a recital and waited. He was glad no one recognized him as he slipped into the back of the theater during the performance to watch her whenever she appeared on stage. He didn't care what was happening in the show because he kept his eyes glued on her. She was as beautiful as he remembered her being. It was too bad that beauty wouldn't last beyond the night, he thought.

Now she was in a pizza joint waiting for her order and talking to a little girl and a man. He was glad that she'd declined the invitation from several of her friends to dine with them after the recital. He was able to catch part of the conversation when he'd hidden in one of the closets right outside of the dressing rooms. He was inches from snatching her then, but there were too many people around. He decided to follow her home and maybe pretend to rear-end her car so that she would get out and then he'd have his chance to grab her, hopefully without anyone noticing.

Lucky for him he didn't need to do that. As she left the theater, she headed in the direction of the pizza place a block away. Since she'd parked her car the block down and walked, he would wait for her to exit and when she walked past the dark alley toward her car, he would pull her into it and drag her into his car. The street was crowded with people, but if he played his cards right and timed it exactly, he could pull her into the alley without anyone noticing.

While she continued to talk and wait for her food, Max crossed the street and waited for her in the alley. His hands shook nervously at the idea of being close to her again. Maybe he would be able to convince her that she'd made a huge mistake breaking up with him and if she gave him another chance, he wouldn't hurt her. If she blew him off like old trash, he would stick to his original plan to silence her.

Going into the alley and moving back far enough that no one would see him standing there in all black waiting, he pulled out a small mirror and held it out toward the street facing the pizza place. This way he'd be able to see her as she walked toward him and at the right moment, he'd grab her and he'd be closer to finally getting what he wanted most; *her.*

**

Kevin was clearing away their discarded food and trash when the man behind the counter shouted that a woman was being attacked on the street.

He didn't hesitate a moment as he leaped into action running for the door and shouting for the man to call nine one-one and telling his mother and Casey to stay put until he returned.

When he reached the sidewalk, he saw a man struggling to pull Michelle into the alley next to the pizza store. He ran toward them.

"Police!" he shouted as he drew the weapon that had been concealed in his back. "Let the woman go," he shouted loudly.

The man turned at the sound of Kevin's voice

and before he could get to him, the man shoved Michelle into the concrete wall and he watched as she first hit the wall with such force that she bounced off of it and then slammed to the ground. The man, who was wearing a black mask and covered in all black, took off running. Kevin started to run after him, but he didn't want to leave Michelle lying on the ground unattended. He went over to her to check to be sure she was okay. The force of the push into the wall and her falling to the ground had knocked her out cold. After checking to be sure he could get a good pulse, he reached for his cell phone and dialed nine one-one himself.

"This is detective Kevin Garner of the ninetieth precinct. I'm at the location of a woman who has been attacked and I need any officers in the area to be on the lookout for a man in all black wearing a black mask running fast."

Kevin gave the information on their location and the direction in which the man had run. He also checked to see if a call had come in from the pizza place. The operator told him one had and officers and an ambulance were on the way. He could hear sirens heading toward him. He stayed with Michelle not letting her go. He didn't know her well, but felt the need to protect her as much as he could, especially since others started walking up to them to see what happened.

When the ambulance and the other officers arrived, Kevin moved the crowd back as the paramedics attended to Michelle. They informed him that she would be alright and that she was actually coming to already.

He watched as they worked to get her on a stretcher and into the ambulance. He took the time to give the officers all of the information he knew, including Michelle's name.

One of the officers who knew Kevin walked up to him.

"Do you think it's the attacker who's been attacking women all over the city?" he asked.

"I don't think so. I think I heard him say her name when he was running away. I think I heard him say 'I'll be back, Shelly' and then he ran off beyond that crowd you see down the street. I know her name is Michelle, but Shelly may be a nickname which means it's someone who knows her. I would have gone after him, but I couldn't leave her lying here, unattended," he said.

"Understandable. Who is she? Do you know her personally?" the officer asked.

"She's a dance instructor. I took Casey and my mom to a dance recital a few blocks away and she was the person who coordinated the recital."

Kevin reached inside of his jacket and withdrew his copy of the program from the recital and handed it to the officer.

"There is information about her in this program. Casey and I had just finished talking to her inside the pizza place when the guy behind the counter shouted someone was being attacked outside. I ran out without knowing it was her. I told him I was a cop and drew my weapon which is when he shoved her against the wall so hard she passed out," he explained. "I hope she's going to be alright," he said as he watched the paramedics race to get back in the cab of the ambulance to get Michelle to the hospital. He ran over to catch them before they left.

"What hospital are you taking her to?" he asked.

Kevin jotted down the information before going back into the pizza place to check on his mother and daughter.

"Kevin, what happened out there?" his mother asked, frightened.

He looked at Casey while he thought about how to approach the subject so that he didn't scare her.

"Michelle, the lady that Casey and I were just talking to was attacked right on the corner."

Kevin saw fear show up on Casey's face. He pulled her closer to him.

"Don't worry she's going to be alright. I'm going to take you both back to grandma's house while I go to the hospital to check on her," he said.

"I want to go check on her too daddy. Can I please go with you?" Casey pleaded.

Kevin didn't see any real harm in that. If he took them with him, then he could go check on Michelle a lot quicker.

"Yes, but you stay close to grandma okay?"

"Yes daddy," she said.

With them in tow, he rushed to get to his car.

**

Michelle was groggy and unaware of where she was. It took her a few minutes to realize she was at the hospital. She remembered being at the pizza place and then getting accosted right after she stepped outside of it. She also remembered going in and out of consciousness and hearing the sound of sirens. She moved a little and the pain hit her like a ton of bricks. Her head and her body ached. She opened her eyes wider and looked around the hospital room and saw a nurse writing something down at a table and when she looked further around the room, she also saw the man from the pizza restaurant that had the beautiful little girl with him. She remembered his name was Kevin. When she moved, she saw him come closer to her.

"Don't try to move too much," Kevin said when he saw her trying to sit up.

"What happened to me?" Michelle asked as she settled back down on the bed to lessen the pain she was feeling.

"After you left the store, some guy attacked you. He shoved you into a wall when I came out and announced that I was a police officer."

"You're a police officer?" she asked, looking perplexed.

"I'm a detective actually."

"Well then I'm glad you were close by. Who knows what would have happened if you hadn't come out to help."

"It's no problem. I'm just glad you're okay. We weren't able to catch the guy and there are some officers who are here waiting to talk to you if you're up for it. They need to get as much information from you as they possibly can."

"Okay."

"Let me go let them know you're awake. Also, my daughter Casey is going crazy with worry over you. Is it okay if she comes in for a minute to see for herself that you're okay?" Kevin asked, knowing he shouldn't, but he also knew Casey wouldn't let up on him all evening if he didn't let her see for herself that the dance teacher was fine.

"Sure, I'd love to see her. I'd hate to think that she's frightened over what happened to me. She needs to see that I'm okay."

Kevin liked that. Even though she was the one in the hospital bed after being attacked, she was also concerned at the reaction Casey may be having to the incident.

"I'll let her come in with my mother just for a few minutes while I hunt down the officers. Also, is there anyone we need to call, possibly family or friends to come here to the hospital?" he asked before leaving.

"No, my family lives in Virginia and I don't want to worry them unnecessarily since I'm fine. I'll call them after I get home. I would like it if someone could call my best friend. She lives a few doors down from me."

Kevin pulled a pen and notepad from his pocket and wrote down the phone number she gave him and promised to have someone call her.

Michelle leaned back into the bed and was thankful things hadn't turned out worse. The guy who attacked her came out of nowhere. She's normally more alert to her surroundings, but it's possible she was still thinking of the successful recital the children had put on and so she wasn't paying much attention. She knew for a fact that she was slightly distracted by the handsome detective after encountering him in the pizza shop. A few things had been running through her mind that caused her to not focus on what was happening around her as she walked toward her car. The detective was still on her mind when the door opened and Casey hesitantly came into the room.

"Hi Casey," Michelle said trying to ease the strain of worry on Casey's face.

"Hi Ms. Michelle. Are you okay?"

"I'm fine thanks to your daddy. He saved me from a very bad man and now I'm going to be just fine. Your daddy said you were worried about me."

"Yes," Casey replied.

"I'm going to be as good as new in a few days so don't worry okay?"

"Okay. I know Alyssa would miss you if you couldn't teach her anymore. She talks about you all the time at school. She loves to dance in your class."

"You don't take any dance classes, Casey?" Michelle asked trying hard to ease the look of terror on Casey's face.

Casey looked sadly down at the floor and shook her head no.

"My daddy works a lot and when school is over I have to go to my grandma's house."

"I bet you would be a great dancer," Michelle said.

Casey smiled brightly hearing the compliment.

"I would be an awesome dancer," she exclaimed proudly.

Michelle knew that she could help with the problem of Casey not being able to come to the dance class. She would talk to Kevin first to see what he thought of the idea. She hated to see any young child with a desire to dance not being able to do so for reasons beyond their control. Kevin and the officers came into the room just as she was again thinking about him.

"Okay Casey, you have to let Ms. Michelle talk to the officers and we need to let her rest so it's time to go."

"Bye Ms. Michelle. I'm glad you're okay."

"Thank you."

"Mom, take Casey out and I'll join you in a few minutes."

Kevin watched as his daughter waved goodbye to Michelle before leaving the hospital room. When they were gone, he turned his attention back to her.

"One of the officers was able to reach your friend Lila and she's on her way here. She was told that you were okay and to take her time. There's no need for her to join you in a hospital bed because she's speeding to get here and ends up in a crash.

These officers are going to get any information from you that you can remember about the incident and we're going to try our best to find this guy. I'm going to give you some privacy and take Casey and my mom home. I'll have the officers brief me on the discussion with you and we'll get some feet on the ground looking for him," he explained.

"Kevin, before you go, I was wondering if I could speak with you in private for a minute before you leave."

Kevin didn't know what she wanted to speak to him about, but it didn't matter to him. He was just happy to spend a little more time with her. He had been enraged when he walked out and saw that the person being attacked was Michelle. He wished he could have caught the guy before he got away, but his immediate concern was for her.

"Sure," he replied as the officers left the room.

"I want to first thank you again for coming to my rescue. I'm normally more careful with knowing my surroundings when I'm out and about alone."

Kevin didn't want her blaming herself for what happened to her.

"I'm just glad I was around to help and don't think that any of this was your fault because you weren't paying attention. It was obvious this guy had a plan and knew what he was doing. He was dressed in all black with a mask. He was ready to attack. Can I ask you one question?" Kevin said.

"Yes."

"Did you know the person who attacked you? Did he say anything to you before I came out that would make you recognize him?"

Michelle thought about what he was saying and realized she couldn't remember anything about the actual attack.

"Not that I can recall. Why do you ask?"

"I thought I heard him say your name before he ran off, but maybe I didn't. Do people call you Shelly?"

Fear set in as she heard the name those closest to her use.

"Family and close friends do. You think whoever this guy is knows me and targeted me?"

"I'm not sure. Everything was happening so fast and for a second I thought I heard him say Shelly."

"I can't think of anyone who would do this to me."

"Let me know if you can recall anything specific about the attack that made the guy seem familiar. I could have been mistaken or it may have been something else. Just think about it and if anything comes to mind, let me know."

"I will. I would hate to think that someone close to me would attack me so brutally."

Kevin hated the thought of that as well.

"There have been a lot of attacks on women around the city lately. We have been trying to catch the person responsible and he could also be responsible for the disappearance of several other women. I'm questioning that a little because I thought I heard him say your name."

Kevin shook all thoughts of that possibility off and concentrated on the fact that they needed to get as much information from her as they could while things were still fresh on her mind.

"Let's get the interview started before they fill you with more medication that will undoubtedly make you sleepy. Anything you can remember will be helpful and don't try to remember everything right now. More will come to you over the next several days and we'll talk more then," he said.

"Okay, but before you call them back in I wanted to thank you somehow for helping me," she said.

"Michelle, I told you, no thanks is necessary."

"I know, but this is nothing big. I teach a dance class each day after school for different age groups. I teach Casey's age on Mondays and Thursdays and I would love for her to join my class. It appears she really wants to dance."

Kevin wished he could accommodate that, but his schedule was too erratic to consider that right now.

"I know Casey would love that, but as a detective I have the worse schedule. I'm working on making some changes so that I can include more after school activities for Casey, but I just can't at the moment. Thank you for thinking about her."

Michelle knew she hadn't seen a wedding ring on his finger at the restaurant, but that didn't mean he wasn't married. She just hoped he wasn't.

"What about your wife? Couldn't she help?" she asked.

Kevin hesitated when Sharon's face crossed his mind.

"I'm not married anymore. Casey's mom died a few years ago so I'm raising Casey alone with help from my mother who watches Casey in the evenings when I'm still at work." He decided to not go into detail about what happened to Sharon.

"I'm sorry for your loss, but I still think this can be worked out. I have a van that picks some of the kids up from school to bring them to class. After class the driver and the assistant drops the kids off at home or the parents pick them up if they can get to the studio before six in the evening. What if I was able to have them pick Casey up at school as well on Mondays and Thursdays and she can then be dropped off at your mom's or at home or you could come pick her up much later than you would right after school? Would that work?"

That would be the answer to his prayers of being able to get Casey involved in activities with other children after school and he would be Casey's hero if he could make this work.

"That would work out fine and I'll pay whatever the fee is for everything. I could work out things with my mother to be available when the van drops Casey off. If I'm already off, I'll swing by and pick her up. Where do you teach your classes?" Kevin asked.

"I have a studio just a few short blocks from where the recital was held which is not far from the elementary school."

Sounded like a great plan to him especially since they didn't live far from the recital location. He thought about it for a few minutes before deciding that he could at least give it a try. He would do anything to make his daughter happy.

"Okay, I'm in. I think Casey will soon be the happiest little girl in the world when I tell her about this," Kevin said excited himself.

"I can't wait to have her in my class. I can see her eyes light up every time she mentions dance."

"You should have seen her at the recital. She could barely contain herself and several times I saw her imitating the dance moves the kids were doing. She loves the stuff."

"I remember being just like her when I was that little and once my parents saw how serious I was about it and how happy taking dance classes made me, they realized the sacrifice was well worth it and besides, look at me now," she said.

Looking at her was exactly what Kevin was doing and though beaten and bruised, she still looked beautiful.

"Well don't look at me now because I'm a mess, but I'm the dancer I always wanted to be and I'm living my dream operating my own studio. You never know how far Casey will go with dance. I'll be excited to see her potential. Why don't you give me your number, if that's okay, and I'll give you a call once I get out of here and I'll tell you everything you need to know? There is no class for a couple of weeks due to some upgrades and expansions of my space that are being done, but I can let you know when classes will resume. Again, it should only be a couple of weeks."

"What if you aren't feeling better by then?" he asked.

"Oh, I'm not the only instructor. I have several college students who help me out with each class. If I'm not up to teaching, they will all pitch in. Besides, by then I'm sure I'll be up and moving about with no problem. I'm in a play myself soon so I have to be ready for that."

Kevin reached in his pocket for his wallet to give Michelle one of his business cards and wrote his personal number on the back.

"Here is my card and my personal cell number is on the back. Are you going to be okay getting home?"

"I'm sure Lila and I will make out fine getting me home and besides, according to the nurse who was in here earlier, they want to keep me overnight for observation. When it's time for me to go home, I'll be fine."

"Sounds like you have this all worked out. Let me know about all of the things Casey will need and I'll make sure I get them before her first class. Thank you for suggesting this."

"I look forward to working with her."

Michelle smiled and Kevin smiled back, glad she was going to be fine and even happier that he was going to see her again. He didn't remember seeing a wedding ring on her finger so he hoped he wasn't getting his hopes up to then only be shot down by her stating she was married. He wouldn't ask now, but he would bring it up when he saw her again. Since she had him call a friend and not a boyfriend or a husband he felt sure she wasn't married. He was hoping she wasn't involved with anyone. Even though he was going against his better judgment showing interest in someone who was a victim of a crime he'd be investigating, there was no way he was going to pass up an opportunity to find out more about her on a personal level.

"I'm going to get out of the way and let these officers do their job. You have my card and if you need anything, just call me.

Kevin left Michelle to be interviewed and to hopefully get some rest. He smiled when he saw his mother and Casey waiting for him. He couldn't wait to get home and tell Casey she would be taking dance lessons. Now that the situation with Casey and dance lessons was taken care of, he would be able to focus on the nut that attacked Michelle and as much as he didn't want to admit it, he believed Michelle's attack was more personal and possibly not related to the other attacks around the city. He was sure he'd heard her attacker say her name. To be safe, he would keep an eye on people he noticed around her taking note of any strange behavior since he'd be seeing her whenever he stopped to pick Casey up from class.

The Dancer - 7

"Michelle, are you sure you don't want to call your family and tell them what happened to you? They'll be worried at first, but they'll be fine once they know you're okay."

"There's no need to worry them Lila. If I tell them, I'll look up and see my entire family running through the door ready to take me back to Virginia. I'm going to be fine once the bruising goes away."

"I'm sure they will, but I still think you need to let them know what happened to you. They have a right to be concerned and worried. Someone attacked you and if that detective had not come to your rescue, who knows what that lunatic would have done to you. I get chills thinking about what you must have gone through. I'm glad you're okay and for the next few days I don't want you to do anything but relax like the doctor said."

"I don't plan on doing anything because I need

to rest up so that I can be ready for the last of my rehearsals next week for the show."

Michelle was preparing for a major Broadway production where she had the star ballerina role. The timing of the rehearsals and the show were perfect since her studio was still closed due to renovations that were being done. The show was running for a few weeks in New York City before it went on the road with other dancers. The studio will open back up before then and her other instructors will keep things going until she returns.

"Do you think you'll be ready to resume dancing by then?" Lila asked.

"Oh, definitely. I feel fine with the exception of a few aches and pains. The attack was over a week ago and this additional week of relaxing will be good for me."

"What are the police saying about the attack? Have you spoken with them again?"

"Not since a few days ago. I spoke with a female officer by phone and answered more of her questions. She said a detective would be stopping by this week to talk to me about the case and to again walk me through that night to see if I missed any details that could help with the investigation."

"Do they seem optimistic that they'll find the person responsible?"

"I don't know yet. So far all they've done is ask a lot of questions and not really shared much. I'm assuming it's because they still don't know much other than it may be linked to other attacks similar to mine that have been happening around the city."

"You were lucky that detective was there to rescue you. Who knows what would have happened to you if he hadn't been there."

"You're right about that and I understand that the police have also been investigating the disappearance of several other women and they're trying to see if it's related to what happened to me. They were dancers as well, though not the same kind of dancer as me. They were strippers and so far there are no leads as to what happened to them. They seemed to have disappeared into thin air. I hope they find those women soon and also find the guy who attacked me so that he can't attack anyone else."

"I agree with you on that. Is that same detective the one who'll be stopping by to interview you this week? He sure was cute from what I saw of him when you were in the hospital."

Michelle looked up from scrolling through text messages on her cell phone.

"Lila are you serious? Did you go from talking about my attack to how fine the detective was? Down girl! Get those hormones in check," she laughed.

"Wait a minute. I did not say he was fine. I said he was cute. You were checking him out too I see."

Michelle blushed realizing she had been caught.

"I didn't say that Lila. I was talking about how

you can easily jump from the conversation about the attack to how fine a guy is and yes he is cute."

"Oh no you don't," Lila said coming over to the sofa to sit down for more personal conversation about the detective.

Michelle played it off like she had no idea what Lila was talking about.

"I can't find the last text message from the producer so that I can let him know I'll be ready in time for the last week of dress rehearsals. I thought I used my cell phone when I must have used the cell phone for the business. I need to go up to my room to get it," Michelle said moving to get up.

"Don't even try changing the conversation. So you did find the detective attractive? What's his name?"

"His name is Detective Kevin Garner and yes I did find him attractive. A woman would have to be blind to not notice how attractive he is and even then, I think she would sense it."

"Girl, go ahead and get you some then! There's nothing wrong with mixing a little pleasure with business. You're probably growing cobwebs on that stuff you have it sealed so tight these days."

"It's not that bad so stop exaggerating. Just because I'm not giving mine away with a coupon and a soft drink like you are doesn't mean cobwebs are growing."

"I say if he's the detective handling your case, you need to find out if he's interested."

"Leave it to you to always have your mind on the bedroom."

"Bedroom, living room, kitchen, hell I'll even take the backseat if the sex is really good. Sometimes you have to get it when you want it and you could be anywhere when that happens. You know I don't pass up a chance to get mine. Now, if for any reason you're not interested in the fine detective, let me know and I'll make my move."

Michelle knew Lila wasn't joking about making a move on the detective. There were times when she wished she was as bold as Lila. Her first move would be to jump the bones of that detective, but she was the reserved one of the two of them. She wouldn't know where to begin. The lingering effects of her relationship with Max had made her more protective over getting involved with anyone.

"I'm not ready to be in another relationship yet."

"Girl, who said anything about being in a relationship. I'm talking about you getting your freak on without thinking about what will happen the next day. Get you some from that sexy detective and keep it moving if you want. You know you want to. I saw the look on your face when I mentioned him. You were already thinking about how sexy he would be naked."

"I was not."

"Stop lying girl. This is me your best friend you're talking to so just admit it."

She didn't want to admit how right Lila was. She

had been thinking about the Kevin ever since the moment she'd seen him in the pizza shop. The fact that he saved her from what the attacker had in mind for her had only heightened her attraction to him. The fact that his handsome face and sexy body were permanently painted in her mind didn't hurt either. What excited her about him most was his walk. He had long, strong legs that had a bit of a curve to them that made her think of long, hot nights of having them cradled around her body. The power and confidence behind his stride had him starring in more than a few of her dreams when she thought about the strength and determination those legs could put behind each and every stroke into her body. Even now, the thought of him had her crossing and uncrossing her legs trying to ease the ache that was growing in between them.

"What is wrong with you girl? You look like you're about to blast off any second with the crossing and uncrossing of your legs. I know the sign and the feeling. What are you thinking about?" Lila asked.

She blushed harder not realizing her reaction to thinking about Kevin was showing in her body movement.

"Nothing."

"Liar," Lila countered. "You were thinking about that detective and if I'm right, you were thinking about him naked, sweaty and wrapped all around you."

"Stop it Lila. "I wasn't thinking about that at all," she lied.

"I don't know why you want to act like I'm the only freaky one in this room. You're always trying to be reserved. I'm telling you being reserved will only result in you having to wipe your own cobwebs away when clearly you want to have Kevin take a trip downtown to clear that thing up!"

"There is no hope for you Lila. Something is seriously wrong with you."

"Yeah, well at least I'm getting mine on the regular and I'm sleeping better than you at night I bet."

"Whatever. Can you warm up the rest of that soup you made yesterday and make me some tea while I call the producer about rehearsals?"

"Anything for you."

Michelle watched as Lila headed toward the kitchen while she got up to look for her other phone. Before she could make it to the stairs the house phone rang. She watched as Lila reached for it before she could.

"Hello," she heard Lila say. "Yes she's here detective. One moment while I get her for you."

She knew something was up when a strange look showed on Lila's face as she turned around.

"Who is it?"

"Well now his timing couldn't be more perfect," Lila said placing her hand over the receiver so that

Kevin couldn't hear her talking about him.

"It's Detective Warner."

Michelle's heart skipped a beat as she nervously paced around straightening her hair and her clothes. After doing so she walked nervously over to grab the phone. As she grabbed for it, Lila shook her head laughing at her.

"What?" Michelle asked.

"He's on the phone not here in person. Why are you fooling with your hair and clothes?" Lila laughed at Michelle's primping.

"Hello Kevin," she said taking the phone and brushing off Lila's teasing.

"Hi, Michelle. I'm calling first to check on how you're doing and then to find out if it's okay if I stop by tomorrow to talk a little more about the attack."

"I'm doing great. I've been home for a week from the hospital and with the exception of a little bruising on my arms and legs, I'm great. I have a little aching, but nothing like it was when I first came home."

"Tell him about your other ache," Lila whispered as she headed to the kitchen.

Michelle shooed her away hoping Kevin hadn't heard her comment.

"I'm glad to hear that. What about my stopping by tomorrow?"

"Tomorrow will be fine. I have a checkup with my doctor, but I should be back home around four in the afternoon. Does that time work for you?" she asked.

"That's perfect. Is there anything I can get you since I'll be coming by? You must need a few things since you've been home all week recovering."

You have no idea what I really need, Michelle thought as the sound of his voice made her think of him naked, sweaty and wrapped around her like Lila said. She shook the thought off and returned her attention to the call.

"Michelle did you hear me?"

"Yes. I'm sorry. No I don't need anything. My friend Lila has been in and out all week taking good care of me, making sure I have the things I need."

"That's great. Do you think you'll be back to dancing soon?"

"I actually have a dress rehearsal for a Broadway show I'm doing soon and I'm sure I'll be ready by then. If all of the bruising isn't gone away, a little make-up will cover that. I just need to get some exercise in to loosen up these bones that have been stiffening up all week."

"Sounds like you're coming along great. I'll let Casey know you're better. She's been worried about you all week."

"Please tell her I'm doing fine and that I said hello. Is she ready for her first lesson next week?"

"Yes she is. The instructor who'll be doing her first couple of classes called yesterday to be sure we had all of the things on the requirements list. Casey has had her bag packed since the day I bought everything. When will you be back to teaching classes?"

"I'm only missing next week's class because of the rehearsal. We're having dress rehearsals all week next week so I had to have fill-ins for my classes, but after that I'll be back to my regular schedule."

"What about the Broadway show? Will that keep you from your classes?"

"No, not at all. All of the classes I teach, including Casey's class, are on Monday and Thursday and those days the play doesn't have an evening showing."

"I see that you have it all planned out. Casey's excitement is through the roof and thanks again for arranging the transportation for her to and from class. My mom will be home when Casey gets in and on the days that I'll pick her up, I'll let you know so that you won't have to worry about putting her on the van."

"I'm glad she's excited and ready. She'll have a lot of fun," Michelle said.

"She's more than excited. I took her to a Broadway show recently and after dinner I gave her a big gift wrapped box. Inside I had placed all of the items for dance class you instructed me to get. At first she didn't know why she was getting it until I told her about the class. The next morning she got up bright and early for school so that she could tell all of her friends that she would be taking classes with you. She's been dancing around the house all week long. Yes I would say she's quite excited."

"I'm glad to hear that. I'm looking forward to getting back in my studio with the kids and to put this whole attack thing behind me."

"I'd like to get my hands on this guy soon. Get some rest Michelle and I'll see you tomorrow."

"I'm glad you'll be handling my case. Before you go can I ask is there any progress on who my attacker is? I know we're going to talk about this tomorrow, but I'm wondering if you had any information you could share. I've been a little worried especially after you said you thought he may have said my name. That could mean it's someone I know."

The last thing Kevin wanted to do was scare her even more than she already was. He felt the need to ease her worry a little so that she wouldn't be consumed with the fact that someone she's been in contact with may have been her attacker.

"At the moment I don't have anything else. My captain wanted to give this case to someone else, but I asked for it. With my being there on the scene, I'm hoping I'll also remember some details that will help the case. I want to be sure whoever this is doesn't get the chance to hurt anyone else. I don't want you thinking too much about what I said about possibly hearing him say your name. In all of the commotion it's possible I didn't hear that, but just thought I did when I realized it was you. Try not to think too much about it and let me take care of keeping you safe."

She felt better hearing his reassurance. There was something about his voice that was slowly drawing her toward him and though something in the back of her mind told her to turn that feeling off and remember that he was the detective working on her case and that even if she were interested, she was sure he wasn't as to not jeopardize her case.

"Thank you Kevin. I appreciate your help. I'll see you tomorrow afternoon."

"Bye Michelle," Kevin said and hung up.

Michelle hung up the phone and ignored the look on Lila's face.

"Don't start Lila. There is nothing there."

"You lie. There is something there. First you start primping like he could see you through the phone and then you smile at the phone as if only the two of you existed. Oh I would say something is definitely there. You are into him and you haven't told me enough about him so give me the rundown on him and don't leave anything out."

"He's a detective Lila and there is nothing to tell."

"Is he handsome? I didn't get a look at his face since I only saw him from behind walking down the hall at the hospital, but from what I saw, he's gorgeous!"

Michelle hesitated not wanting the conversation to continue, but she also knew she needed to tell someone about her attraction to the handsome detective.

"Yes Lila, he is very handsome. He's tall and very, very sexy. He has this amazing cowboy stance that's makes you want to jump him to get the ride of your life. He has a rich, chocolate brown complexion and the sexiest goatee I've ever seen. He is all muscle too and no sign of any body fat. That was easy to tell even with clothes on. When he looks at me, it seems like he can look right into my soul. I can feel him even though he hasn't touched me in an intimate way. I've never had such a reaction to a man before."

"Michelle I have never heard you talk about a man like this before. I've got to meet this mystery man. If he is all that you say he is, don't you dare let him get away. I know you said he has a little girl. Where's the mother?" Lila asked.

"I don't know the circumstances, but he did mention to me that Casey's mother died a few years ago. He didn't share more and I didn't pry."

"Well, I'm sorry for his loss, but that means he may be open to getting to know you better. I told you it was time for you to get back out there."

Lila may be right that it was time for her to get back in the dating arena. She wouldn't get her hopes up high. She would just wait to see if Kevin feels any kind of spark about her as she's been feeling about him. She hoped the interest was mutual and that the fact that he was working on her case wouldn't dissuade him from showing a true interest in her.

Lila then turned serious again.

"Are you sure you're okay? I know you told me what happened, but we haven't really talked about it."

"I'm fine. I do have one thing I want to tell you that Kevin mentioned. He said he thought he heard my attacker say my name. You know about this person who has been assaulting women lately and he still remains at large. Kevin thought it may be this person who also attacked me, but he swears he heard the guy say my name. I didn't hear anything because by then I had already passed out. When he first accosted me, he didn't say anything. He just placed his hand over my mouth and started pulling me towards the alley. He had on very big, thick gloves so I couldn't get a scream out. Luckily the man in the pizza place could see what was happening out of his front window. Suppose it was someone who knows me? I can't think of anyone, but suppose that's the case? I don't know what I should do about that. I can't live in fear Lila. I'm really hoping Kevin was wrong and the attack was just a random one."

Michelle held her stern, serious face for a few minutes while Lila processed everything she'd said.

"Michelle, suppose it is someone you know. Suppose it was Max," Lila said with hesitation. She didn't want to bring up the obvious, but since no one knew where Max was, maybe it was possible he was still in the New York area and had begun stalking Michelle again.

"Believe me. I thought about that. As soon as Kevin said he thought the man had said my name I immediately thought of Max. Even at his worse, I can't imagine him hurting me like that. I don't know. I'm thinking Kevin didn't hear the man say my name. I believe it may have been the same person who has been attacking other women. Hopefully they'll get a suspect and arrest him before he has a chance to hurt anyone else," Michelle said.

**

After he disconnected the call Kevin stared at his phone.

"What am I doing?" he said to no one in particular. He knew that he was already crossing a line and couldn't seem to pull himself back from it. He shouldn't have gotten so personal as to say that he was going to take care of keeping her safe. He knew from his many years of training and being on the force that he should always speak in terms of what the department would do to keep her safe and not him specifically. There was something about Michelle that made him want to personally protect her. It wasn't just her beauty that he was attracted to. It was everything about her from her beauty to her personality and kind spirit and especially the way she cared so much about Casey being able to fulfill her dream of taking dance. He liked how caring she was and if the circumstances were different and he weren't the detective handling her case, he would work on being a lot more personal with her, but that wasn't to be so now. He had a job to do and he could only get it done with a clear head. He needed to get himself in check before visiting her because if he didn't, there was no telling how far over the line he would go with no strength to cross back over.

**

Max paced back and forth in the alley behind the club where his latest version of Shelly worked. He didn't want to be here tonight, but he needed a stand-in for the failed attempt he'd made at finally having Shelly in his grasp. If it hadn't been for that nosey police officer who had intervened the night he'd almost had her, he could be reading about her demise in the newspaper already and seeing her beautiful face sprawled across every television news channel.

Knowing that Shelly was still alive to haunt his every waking moment is the cause for his being out again at yet another vile club full of more women who would undoubtedly turn him down for anything that didn't involve him paying money for their time.

Ever since he missed his chance with Shelly, his hands have not stopped shaking. He knew they wouldn't until he was able to get them around her neck, squeezing the life and breath out of her body.

While he planned his next attempt, he needed a stand-in Shelly again and as luck would have it, as he waited outside of the club, he saw his next Shelly enter through the side door.

The Dancer - 8

"I know that's not what you're wearing when the detective gets here," Lila said seeing the old, plain Jane black pants and churchy white shirt Michelle had on.

Michelle looked down at her appearance.

"What's wrong with what I have on?" she asked perplexed. She thought she looked fine.

"I swear it's like you've never been around a hot man before. This man is the finest man you and I have ever seen. You know you like him, you know you want him and if you're going to get the man, you have to put out the right bait. Go change."

Michelle turned and gave her friend an evil eye.

"Girl I am not trying to snag the detective. He's coming over here to interview me, not take me out on a date."

"Well if you play your cards right you'll get a date out of it, so go change."

"No, I think I look fine."

"You look like you're going in to an office for work. Go put on something more comfortable. I'll go grab something for you," Lila said heading for the stairs.

Michelle stopped her.

"You will do no such thing. I can go get my own clothes," she said giving in, knowing Lila would never let up.

"Good. Put on a skirt and a comfortable top, the kind you always wear when you're lounging at home. Get comfortable."

"Yeah, yeah," Michelle said heading to the stairs to her bedroom to change. She wasn't surprised when Lila followed behind her.

After trying on a few items, she finally found something different, but not too inviting.

"How is this?" she asked Lila, showing her the black flowing skirt and pink and while tank top.

"That looks fine. Now go down and relax until he gets here so that you don't look like you've been anxiously waiting for him to show up."

"You are such the mother hen."

Michelle walked passed her friend to the stairs. She did as Lila asked and made herself comfortable on the sofa in front of the television.

"Do you need me to hang around while the detective is here?"

"No, I'll be fine. Since I'm moving around fine and he's just coming to get more information about what I remember, I'll let you off duty from taking care of me for now."

They laughed, lightening the mood.

"Okay, what time is he coming?"

Before Michelle could respond her front door buzzed. She stood nervously staring at the door, not being able to move. Her heart sped up and her hands felt sweaty as she wiped them on her skirt.

"Shelly you are pathetic. Just mount the guy will you and get it over with!" Lila said laughing as she went to open the door.

"Hello detective," she heard Lila say. As soon as she did, he came fully into the room. He was tall and broad making the room seem smaller with his presence. He looked as sexy as he did the first time she'd seen him. As he came toward her and smiled, her heart skipped a beat. His electric smile took his sexiness to a whole new level.

"You look like you're healing well," Kevin said. He knew she looked even more beautiful than she had before, but he didn't want to cross a line by mentioning that. She was in fact more beautiful than he remembered.

Kevin felt his body react to her and he willed it to calm down.

"Thank you. I am doing much better than I was. You remember my friend Lila?"

Kevin turned to again acknowledge her presence.

"I do. She must be taking good care of you

because you're up and moving around."

"I was tired of lying around and it's time to get my body moving around and ready to get back to work soon. The kids are missing me and I miss them. Please come in and have a seat."

"Shelly unless you need something else, I'm going to get out of here."

"I'm good. Thanks Lila. I'll call you later."

Michelle waited until she heard the door shut and lock before she turned her attention back to her guest.

"I'm not sure how much additional information I have for you. I've told you and the other detectives what I remembered."

"Well sometimes after a few days a few more details may come to mind and I wanted to capture them while they may be fresh. Are you ready for some intense questioning?"

"I sure am. Do you want anything to drink while we talk?"

Kevin looked at her, not blinking, mesmerized by her beauty. He had to remember he was with her for business purposes.

"Maybe some water?" he asked. He certainly could use it to cool off.

"Water it is," Michelle said getting up.

**

After questioning Michelle for over an hour, Kevin was tired of talking himself. He also knew that coming by to talk to her today was a good idea. She had provided him with information about her activities that day and though she didn't see anyone following her or watching her, she mentioned she'd had a strange vibe all week as if someone had been following her. A few times she thought she saw someone across the street from her house watching her, but nothing ever came of it. There are always people out walking the streets in her neighborhood.

She had also given him information about her last relationship which gave him some concern. She hadn't given it much thought because she had not heard from the guy in a while, but that didn't mean that he hadn't come back around to scare her and he was going to look into it and try and track down this Max guy.

He checked his watch and realized he was off for the day and looked forward to going home and relaxing without having work on his agenda or his mind. For now he wanted to enjoy a little more time talking to Michelle.

"I hope I didn't tire you out with all of my questions?" he asked.

"Not at all since I'm hoping all this information gathering turns into a benefit for the case. I know the police are looking into any links with the other missing women, wondering if they are related."

"I've been doing some checking and it turns out there are four missing cases that appear to be linked together, especially with the fact that they are all dancers. The difference in their missing cases and your attack is that they were strippers and you're a professional dancer. I'm going to keep digging to see what I can find out, but not tonight. I'm planning to turn work off and enjoy my first weekend off in a long time with Casey."

"How is Casey?" Michelle asked.

"She's great. She's the perfect little girl. She asks me about you daily. I didn't tell her I was coming by to interview you today because would be full of questions when I got home later," he laughed.

"She's a beautiful girl. She looks a lot like you."

Kevin smiled loving how they turned the conversation away from work to more personal.

"A lot of people say that until they see pictures of her mother. She is the spitting image of her."

"Her mother must have been very beautiful."

Kevin hesitated before responding.

"She was."

There was a deafening silence after the mentioning of Casey's mother and Michelle didn't like the somber look that appeared on his face so she changed the subject to something lighter.

"What do you and Casey have planned for the night?"

"No real big plans. I promised her a night of Disney movies and pizza with extra toppings. What are your plans for the evening since you look like you're doing better?"

"I'm going to stay in the weekend and workout.

I have a studio downstairs with some equipment. I need to build strength up in my legs. I'm not used to sitting around for a week without some type of dancing or exercise and my body is not getting the workout I want it to have."

The moment the words exited her mouth, Michelle realized the double meaning behind her words. She hoped Kevin didn't catch it. When she looked over at him, she had a sneaky suspicion his mind went where hers did as well and she blushed before looking away. She was glad that he didn't point out the obvious from her response.

Kevin was about to say something about the meaning he got from her words, but stopped himself. He was attracted to her and though he was now off the clock and on his personal time, he didn't want to make her uncomfortable. He spoke up anyway, not being able to keep it in.

"Workout or not, your body is incredible and doesn't appear to need any extra work."

Her pulse quickened. His words were music to her ears. It appears he was just as attracted to her as she was to him.

"Thank you," she said turning back to look into his gorgeous eyes. They were magnetic. She didn't know what else to say besides thank you.

They sat with no one speaking, but the clear sound of their mutual increased breaths was evident to her. She figured he must be struggling with his attraction to her as she was with hers for him. They were obviously trying to keep things professional, but the electricity in the air could not be denied.

Michelle watched Kevin move, in what seemed like slow motion, as his hand reached out to caress her cheek.

"You are so beautiful," he said.

Michelle knew any moment she would pass out from the excitement of feeling his hand touch her face. She was so in tuned with him that she would have accepted him touching any part of her body if it meant being closer to him.

"I apologize if I'm crossing a professional line here, or any line for that fact. I didn't know what else to say besides the truth and what was on the tip of my tongue."

At the mentioning of his tongue, Michelle looked from his eyes to his mouth and felt a fire building up in her body. It was one that made her want to reach out and touch him just as he was doing. As he continued to caress her cheek, moving his hand down to caress around her neck, her stomach did a little dance and her mouth went dry.

"Michelle, tell me to stop and I will. I don't want you to feel uncomfortable because that's the last thing I would ever do. I'm struggling with sitting here next to you without touching you in some way."

Michelle figured since truth was on the table, she'd add a little of her own.

"Truth is I was hoping you'd touch me or show some sign that you were as attracted to me as I am to you. I didn't think that I should be since you're working on my case, but I can't seem to help myself. I can tell you are a remarkable man and any woman would be lucky to have your interest."

"It's been torture sitting here next to you and not giving in to the feeling of wanting to be as close to you as I could get without being inappropriate. Believe me when I say being this attracted to any woman has never, ever happened to me before. It's never been as instantaneous as it has been with you."

She was relieved knowing what was happening was a two-way street.

"I'm glad to know it's not just me who was feeling that way. Would you believe me if I said I've been tortured since the moment I met you at the recital? I know it didn't seem obvious, but it's the truth."

He slid a little closer to her on the couch.

"So you don't mind my being this close to you and touching you?"

She slid a little closer to him.

"Not at all."

As she drew closer, she hoped the caress of her cheek and neck would lead to more than just that. She watched as Kevin's face moved closer to hers and she knew she was about to get her wish and she welcomed it.

She looked into his dark, piercing eyes as they appeared to darken even more giving them an erotic look, drawing her in even more. Before she could breathe her next breath, he leaned in just a whisper away from her lips, seemingly waiting for her to come the rest of the way so that he would know she wanted what was about to happen as much as he did. When she did, the next feeling made the blood first rush to her head and to the lower part of her body which was now burning with excitement for him. He kissed her and thoughts of anything but him escaped her as she focused only on him and the feel of his lips on hers.

The kiss had an unexpected feeling on him. Kevin knew it would be good, but he had no idea of the impact it would have. The first touch of his lips to hers made the room spin and his mind transfixed on all of the things he'd like to do to her following the kiss. What started out as a soft kiss with a soft tug on Michelle's lips turned into one of fiery passion the moment their lips met. He'd planned to just get a taste of her incredible, supple lips, but one feel of them made him lose control and he dove in for more than a light kiss.

Michelle was caught up and didn't know what was happening to her as she opened up for him. Though she had a feeling he meant to keep the kiss light and gentle, it turned into a probing of tongues as they dueled trying to get as much out of the kiss as they could draw. She joined in the onslaught by reaching her arms up and around Kevin's neck, pulling him toward her as she felt him mold his mouth to hers to the point that anyone watching them wouldn't be able to see where she started and where he ended.

Kevin's tongue felt as if it was swollen as he ventured all around the inside of her mouth. The kiss continued on as neither wanted to release the mouth of the other. He pulled back a little to suckle around her lips before going back in for more of the tongue that was driving him wild. He didn't know what was coming over him. He couldn't remember the last time he was so aroused. He wanted her in the worse way, but also knew that he had to be careful. He was still the lead detective in charge of her case and he didn't want to compromise anything because he couldn't control the lust that was causing them both to almost claw at each other. When he felt the need to breathe, he broke the kiss off and tried to get his body back in check.

"Wow, that was some kiss," she said.

He couldn't agree more.

"Well I think there is no doubt anymore that we are attracted to each other," he said, breathing as if he'd run a marathon.

"I'd say you are right about that," she agreed.

Kevin wasn't ready to stop yet. He looked at her lips which appeared swollen from his kiss and couldn't deny what he wanted.

"Want more?" he said.

Michelle didn't know if he was asking her if she wanted more or if he was declaring that he wanted more. Either way, the answer to both assumptions was yes. She knew that it was inevitable that they wouldn't be able to stop after a kiss like that. Yeah, she wanted much, much more.

"Yes," she said and this time she took the lead by reaching out and gripping his face between her hands. Her focus was on the lips that had already brought her body more pleasure than she'd ever experienced. Feeling daring, she stuck her tongue out and ran it along the seam between his lips. She felt enthralled and erotic when he moaned at her intimate caress. That moan made her feel bolder than she ever remembered being around a man and she probed his lips until he opened them for her. Once inside she didn't let up as she sought out his tongue, knowing the reaction her body would have to tasting him once again. She went in over and over not caring that she wasn't soft or gentle, but hard and demanding drawing from him everything she'd ever needed in a kiss from a man, but had been too shy over the years to go for it. She liked that he didn't hesitate to respond.

Kevin didn't want to think of the consequence of being in Michelle's house, on her couch devouring her mouth with a kiss that was destined to lead to more. He couldn't pull back because as much as he wanted and needed to gain control of the situation, he couldn't deny the want and need he felt Michelle needed in return from him. Before he knew what was happening, he pulled her up gently onto his lap for an even more intimate connection. He was careful not to cause her further pain, knowing that she was probably still experiencing discomfort from the attack.

Michelle sighed in relief the moment Kevin lifted her to his lap. As the kiss went on as if neither needed to take a breath, she couldn't stop her legs from twitching and rubbing against each other searching out relief for the ache between them. She clung to his mouth as if she needed to hold on because her life depended on it. She wiggled ever more when she felt Kevin's hands on her legs, shifting her skirt higher and higher.

Kevin knew he shouldn't, but his hands had a life of their own as they caressed first her ankles, then her lower legs, which led up to her upper legs and when he wanted to slip his hands between them to open them up so that he could go even further, he didn't need to. Michelle opened her legs for him wanting the invasion as much as he did.

The minute he reached the seam of her panties and rubbed up and down, he thought Michelle would leap off of his lap. The wetness he felt and the way her legs moved, let him know that she needed relief and he knew he couldn't stop unless he gave it to her.

He opened her legs wider so that she knew what his intent was. He reached his hand back up and the moment he encountered her soaking wet panties again, he moved them to the side and slipped one finger inside of her without warning. He got the reaction he wanted when she tried to leap out of his lap. He used his other arm to steady her while his fingers moved in and out of her making her break the kiss in order to exhale.

"Oh my," she said. "That feels good."

"It feels good to me too. Enjoy it baby," he said softly into her ear. After speaking he snaked his tongue out and lightly licked and kissed her earlobe causing her body to thrash around on his lap. He focused as much attention on her ear with his tongue as he was doing with his fingers between her legs, stroking her with a gentle, probing motion bringing her to the brink where he knew she was seconds from an explosive release.

Michelle tried to go back to kissing Kevin, but her body was climbing to heights unknown to her. Her body was out of control and she didn't know what to do with her lips or her hands as her mind clouded with the feeling of euphoria. Her release was imminent.

"Yes, yes! Don't stop," she wantonly screamed as her release slammed into her. She thrashed around like a woman out of her mind as Kevin's penetrating finger was joined by a second as he gave her even more.

"I wouldn't dream of it baby. Let go and take what you need. I'm not stopping until your body is exhausted."

Michelle screamed through her release and as her body was about to calm down, she realized a second orgasm was already on the horizon. That had never happened to her before. Kevin's fingers were magically doing things to her that she hadn't expected.

"It's happening again," she screamed, this time into his ear as she laid her head on his shoulder while gripping him for support.

"I know, I feel it so don't hold back. Come on and give me more. I already feel your essence running down my fingers and I want to feel more," he whispered in her ear.

His words mixed with the feeling of his fingers sent her over the edge once again. This time she screamed into his neck as her body rocked and shook from the quake that never seemed to end. She rode out the pleasure until her body began to quiet and she fell limp in his arm.

When her body finally calmed down, Kevin removed his hand from in between her legs and pulled her tighter to him, covering her face with kisses.

"You are so incredible and so responsive to me. I couldn't resist touching you and I never want to stop."

Michelle knew if she could speak, she would agree, but right now, she needed to find the strength to breathe normally again.

She didn't know what to do next. Here she sat in the lap of a man who came to her house to interview her about her attack and she ended up having two of the best orgasms of her life right in a row. She was quite sure she could have experienced a third, but not sure she could have done so without passing out. Now that she was coming down from her high, doubt and shame started to set in. A few minutes earlier, she was excessive with want, need and desire and couldn't get enough of Kevin's touch and now she wondered what he thought about how easy it was for him to be able to touch her the way that he did without any resistance from her. He must think she's like this with all men and that would be far from the truth. She needed to lift her head, but at the moment, she was feeling shameful.

Kevin sensed a change in Michelle's body. Where she was soft, pliant and willing a few minutes ago, her body now felt tense, edgy and nervous.

"Michelle, are you alright? Talk to me," he said concerned that she may now be regretting what just happened. Even now his body was still hard for her and he would like nothing better than to divest them both of every stitch of clothing and sink himself into her supple body, but he would save that for another day if given the chance. He wanted what just happened between them to be about her and the need he felt in her and not about his needs. He willed for his body to calm down so that they could talk through whatever was going through her mind.

"Michelle, please say something."

"I don't know what to say," she replied, not bothering to lift her head from his shoulder.

"Tell me I didn't do something wrong here."

That got a rise out of her and she sat straight up.

"You did nothing wrong. I wanted you to touch me as much as you wanted to and I enjoyed every minute of it. I was beginning to feel ashamed of what you would think about me allowing you to touch me like this considering we don't know each other besides the little we've shared while you're looking into my attack. I don't want you to think something like this is the norm for me. I've never been like this before. Being around you brought something out of me."

Kevin felt the need to reassure her that her worries were for naught.

"I could never think anything bad about what we just experienced. You are an exquisite, desirable, gorgeous woman and there should be no shame about what we shared. This was incredible and I don't see it as anything negative at all."

Michelle smiled and he knew everything would be alright.

"So what now?" she asked, wiggling a little on his lap, letting him know she could feel his long, thick erection pressing against her behind.

He smiled realizing she'd gotten back into a

comfort zone with him.

"I would say I would love to take this to a bed, but unless you have protection, we'll have to table the next level to another time because I don't have any."

His comment had them both laughing like teenagers.

"You mean, you don't walk around with condoms in your wallet like most men, ready just in case the opportunity presents itself."

Kevin laughed even harder.

"I guess I'm not your typical guy. I'm not involved with anyone so I didn't see a reason to walk around with a wallet full of condoms and though I know we just crossed a line here, this isn't something I have ever done before. This was special, Michelle; you are special and I didn't come prepared to have my hand in your panties or with thoughts of stripping you naked, though I'd love to very much. What do you say, we slow things down a bit. I really like you and I don't want you to think this is what I do all the time or that this is what I came here looking for. I want to see you again, outside of work, as soon as I figure out how to do that without compromising this case. From the moment I saw you at the dance recital, I've had you on my mind. I wanted to ask you out that night, but couldn't find the right opportunity. Now that I have you here sitting in my lap, maybe now is a good time to see if you'd like to spend more time getting to know me."

Michelle threw her head back and laughed.

"I haven't been with a man since my last relationship and if there were any condoms anywhere in this house, they'd be out of date and no good by now. In any other situation I would say we did this backwards since you now clearly know me a little better. I would like nothing better than to get to know you and I don't think it'll have an impact on the case. I already know you are as professional as they come. Now that we're here, where we are, I would love to be able to see you again."

"Whew, that's good to know. Now I can breathe a little better and the next time we're in a situation like this, I will make sure we're prepared for the next step."

"Sounds like a good plan to me."

"Well, I promised Casey a movie and pizza tonight so how about you and I do dinner and a movie tomorrow night if you're up to it?"

"That sounds great and I'd love to. You'd better get going because I'm sure Casey is at the door waiting for you to get home so that you can spend time together."

He didn't want to leave, but Michelle was right. Casey was probably already impatiently waiting at the door.

"Come walk me to the door and lock up. I'll call you tonight if you feel up to it. Casey usually goes to bed at ten on weekends, but she never makes it past the second movie. I'll look up and she'll be out by eleven. Is that too late to call you?" he asked, hopeful.

"I'll be up waiting on your call."

She stood from his lap watching as he stood straightening up his clothes. His still hard bulge was quite evident to them both.

"Would I sound whorish if I said I could help with that?" she said pointing to his hardness.

Kevin tried to adjust himself so that his desire for her was not so obvious.

"Not at all, but I'll be fine. As soon as the night air hits me, everything will be back to normal."

He moved so that they were flush against each other.

"Let me make something very clear though. The next time we're in a situation like this, you can do anything you want to any part of my body. It's all yours for the taking."

Before she could respond, Kevin leaned down and took her mouth in a sizzling kiss that let her know that the best was still yet to come.

The Dancer - 9

"Everyone did a great job in class today," Michelle said to her room full of six, seven and eight year olds. Her class was just wrapping up when she spotted Kevin waiting at the door for Casey. As soon as he noticed that she'd seen him, he gave her a small wave and a bright smile. Michelle shivered at the sight of him looking sexy leaning against the doorway looking at her as if he could devour her from across the room. The man was just too damn sexy and every time she was around him her thoughts got all muddled. While the children played around, she went over to say hello.

"Hi Kevin. You made it in time to see Casey dance I see."

"Yes and I'm so proud of her. She's doing a great job. Every time I come by to watch her, I'm impressed at how good she is."

"Your daughter is certainly a natural. She did an

incredible job with every instruction today."

Kevin looked over at his daughter beaming as she talked with other little girls in the room.

"It's been a long time since I've seen her this happy. Thanks again for the suggestion to get her in the class. I have a feeling this is just what Casey needed," he said.

"I'm happy to hear that. I'm glad I could help."

"You did more than that Michelle," he said while reaching down to bring her hand into both of his.

She looked down at their joined hands and then back up into his handsome face, a face she's getting addicted to looking into. They looked around to see if any of the children were witnessing this display of affection between the two of them. Noticing none of the children were paying attention to them and that all of the children were being looked after by one of Michelle's instructors, they turned back to each other and slowly backed out of the room and into the hall where Kevin pulled her into his arms and kissed her like he hadn't just seen her the night before when he stopped by her house to let her know he'd missed seeing her because he'd been busy at work.

After that day he given her two extraordinary orgasms, they had spent several evenings going out to dinner and really get to know each other. They hadn't been intimate since that first time on her sofa when he'd given her pleasure she hadn't experienced before. When they finally came up for air, she felt all tingly as she did whenever he touched her.

"I needed that," he said still holding her in his arms.

"Feel free to need that whenever you feel like it. In fact, I encourage it," she said.

"I'll take you up on that. What if I take you up on it tomorrow night? The only thing is it may be really late, like after eleven. We're making some progress on the cases of the missing women and I have some leads to follow up on."

Michelle was anxious to know if they were close to getting the person responsible for the disappearance of the women. Already, people were assuming the women were dead because no sign of either of them had surfaced.

"Any word on whether it's connected to my attack?"

"We don't have anything yet that leads us to believe they are connected, but I'm still digging."

"Okay. It makes me nervous thinking someone is still out there and could be harming other women. I'm starting to think it wasn't Max because by now he probably would have surfaced, coming after me again."

"I don't even want to think about that. All signs lead to your attack being random."

"What about your thoughts that you heard him say my name?"

"I've been thinking about that and wondering if

in the heat of the moment, I heard something that wasn't really there. Either way, I'm still keeping my eye on you and I've told you about being safe and if you need to be out late, give me a call."

"I will. I love having a tall, sexy cop having my back."

"It's a pretty back that I don't mind watching. What about tomorrow night?"

"I say I'll be up waiting no matter how late it is. What about Casey?"

"Well, since you said yes, I'm going to let her spend the night at my mom's. That way after spending some time with you, I won't have to stop and pick her up before I go to work the next morning."

Michelle looked at him with longing in her eyes.

"You could come prepared to spend the night and go to work from my house," she said. "It's just a thought."

"Best thought I've heard all day. I better let you get back to your class. I wanted to stop in and check out Casey's dance moves and to get my fill of you to get me through the rest of my shift. I'll call you tonight, sweetness."

Kevin snatched one last kiss before darting back out the door.

**

"I'll be by early in the morning to pick Casey up for school so you don't have to worry about doing that tomorrow."

Kevin looked at his mother as he checked Casey's bag to be sure he packed everything.

"I'll have her ready," she said smiling.

He noticed her strange smile and knew what it was about.

"Go ahead and say it mom."

"I won't say a word," she said. "I'm just glad you're finally getting back on the dating horse. It's been too long. You can't let what happened with Sharon keep you from finding love and happiness again. Sharon was different. I think you know that now. She was very needy. I loved her very much, but I saw the way she needed your attention every hour of every day. With the kind of work you do, you need the kind of woman who will be understanding of the time you are away and have her own interests to occupy her time. Sharon never had that and even after having Casey, it wasn't enough. It's time you lived again and not just living when it comes to Casey. You need your own life, your own personal life as well. Tell Michelle I said hello. How is she since the attack?" his mother asked.

Kevin's mind drifted for a moment to the conversation he'd had earlier at the station with some of the other detectives. They had been doing some investigating into Michelle's attack as well as some other attacks around the city and anything that could link them to the disappearance of several dancers. A few nights ago, another dancer had turned up missing so now the search was on. They now had some type of serial kidnapper or killer on their hands and they upped their game to track down whoever was responsible. As for Michelle's case, they hadn't made much progress and since he had been seeing her, he'd been keeping an extra eye out for anyone who appeared to be watching her and he'd seen nothing.

He tried tracking down the Max guy she had been involved with and so far there was no lead as to where he could be. He knew the guy could be living in another state by now. So far the other attacks were similar to what happened to Michelle and it was possible the same person had attacked her and the other women and the guy's selection of Michelle was a random attack. Either way, they needed to get the creep off the streets so that he couldn't hurt anyone else, especially Michelle.

Kevin was beginning to feel more than just a slight attraction to her. After going out on several dates, he'd come to enjoy the woman he was getting to know and was looking forward to going to bed and waking up next to her. He couldn't until the end of his shift and hoped that nothing came up that would make him have to cancel on his time with her tonight. He'd been looking forward to it since she suggested he stay all night and he was more than ready. He'd been fighting his biggest temptation in not taking her to bed yet. He wanted it to be right and didn't want it to be a spur of the moment thing. He wanted them both to be ready and it appeared she was just as ready as he was.

"Kevin, did you hear me?"

He was snapped out of his thoughts.

"Sorry mom, what did you say?"

"I asked how Michelle was doing since the attack.

"She's doing fine and I'll let her know you asked about her when I see her tonight. I'm going to go say goodnight to Casey. I thought she would have come back down by now to say bye to me. I hear the television going and it must be around five when her favorite shows come on."

"Okay. Tell her to come watch television down here with me while I'm finishing up dinner."

He went in search of his daughter with an extra pep in his step thinking about the night he was looking forward to having with Michelle.

**

"Do you have plenty of condoms and possibly some lube?"

Michelle almost choked on the water she was drinking hearing Lila treat her like she was a spry teenager.

"Lila, stop it. I do not need you giving me advice on safe or kinky sex with your mentioning of condoms and lube in the same sentence."

"I'm just saying make sure you're prepared this time. No more lap action without being able to get to the good stuff!"

"I knew I should have never told you about that night because I knew you'd bring it back up one day. Before you say it again as if I didn't hear it the first time, yes I bought condoms and I'm sure Kevin has them as well. There is no doubt about the intentions for tonight and we're way overdue. Other than some very, very hot kisses and touching, we haven't gone further than that since the couch incident and I'm about to pop," she laughed.

"I hear you. Go ahead and get yours. I'm not mad at you and I won't even ask you to tell me all about it later. I'm just glad you're getting the kinks out. Those cobwebs must itch!"

She laughed at Lila.

"You are truly certifiable Lila. I mean you are mental facility ready."

"All kidding aside, I'm really happy for you. Kevin seems like a great guy and I know you really like him and that the feeling is mutual. He is just what you need in your life to help you forget about that relationship that we will not even speak of. Actually speaking of it, no signs of Max?"

The mentioning of his name made Michelle feel uneasy.

"No word from him and no signs of him either."

"So you've moved on from the idea that it was Max who attacked you?"

"Now that I think about it, I don't think it was him. The guy who attacked me wasn't as big as Max was. This guy was much thinner. You know how big Max was. I'm hoping the few leads they have on some other missing women will lead them to whoever this guy is. As for me, I'm going to get myself ready for my man so I'll talk with you later."

"Alright and make sure you do everything I would do and more."

Michelle laughed without commenting as she hung up her phone. She went in search of the base to put her phone back on and passed by her front window. As she looked out, something caught her eye. For a split second it looked like someone was watching her house from a car across the street. When she looked closer, she was almost sure that whoever was in the car was staring straight at her. She moved as close as she could to the window and as soon as she tried to get a better look, the car took off speeding down the street. She stood stunned for a minute wondering if she was imagining the car's occupant was looking at her or that whoever it was had simply been looking her way before pulling off. She didn't know what to think. She shook it off headed to her bathroom to get a shower before Kevin showed up in a few hours. She couldn't wait to see him.

**

"You look beautiful," Kevin said when she opened the door for him. He'd told her he would be late and didn't expect for her to look so refreshed and wide awake considering it was almost eleven o'clock. He was just lucky to get out of the station before anything came up that needed his attention. As soon as he realized the coast was clear he headed for the door and never looked back. He stopped at home to grab a quick shower and an overnight bag. He'd made sure to check the bag to be sure he remembered the condoms. He had no plans of going half-way with Michelle tonight. He didn't want the lack of protection to keep him from loving her the way he wanted.

"Thank you handsome. You look nice yourself," she said moving so that he could come in. Once she'd locked the door and set the alarm, she turned and was whisked up into Kevin's strong arms where he wasted no time searching out her lips that he loved suckling on at every opportunity. Michelle relaxed into him, wrapping her legs around his waist and her arms around his neck, going at his mouth like a starving woman. As she held on to him, she felt his big, strong hands as they gripped her behind pulling her even closer to him. Her body reacted to the feeling of his erection pressing into the most intimate part of her and she ground her body into him letting him know there was no doubt about her want and need for him tonight.

"Bed," was all she heard him say when he tore his mouth away from hers for a second to speak.

"Yes," was her only reply when he turned toward the steps and headed toward her bedroom, not letting her go as he made his way with her still clinging to him.

Michelle's heart pounded in her chest with every step he took getting them closer to her bed. She couldn't wait to get him naked and the way he was gobbling her up with his kisses, he was thinking the same thing.

Once in her room, Kevin dropped the bag he was still holding over his shoulder onto the bed and slowly lowered Michelle to it.

"Tell me now if you feel the need to talk, watch television or cuddle because my thoughts are on getting inside of you as fast as humanly possible. I've been thinking about making love to you all day and I'm not sure I can wait unless you tell me otherwise."

Michelle said nothing. Instead, she reached up and removed the sundress she was wearing revealing that she was completely naked underneath.

"I'm right with you sweetheart," she said moving toward the center of the bed and watching his reaction. His eyes widened and the protrusion in the front of his pants looked painful being held prisoner behind his straining zipper.

As he reached to remove first his shirt then his pants, Kevin couldn't help but take in the sight before him.

"You are beautiful and you continually surprise me. If I had known you were naked under that dress when I first came in, we never would have made it up the stairs."

Michelle smiled happy that he liked what he saw. She made herself comfortable on the pillows at the top of her bed while she watched him remove the rest of his clothing, marveling at his Adonis physique. She knew hidden beneath under those clothes was a gorgeous beast of a man and he didn't disappoint as he stood before her in boxer briefs that were barely containing his long, thick, turgid flesh. At the sight of him, parts of her stirred that had been waiting for this moment since they'd first kissed on her couch.

After removing his last piece of clothing, Michelle marveled at the sight of him standing before her naked and hard as steel. She crossed and then uncrossed her legs trying to find a way to alleviate the pressure that was building between them.

Before he joined her on the bed, he reached into his bag and withdrew the condoms he brought for the night before tossing the bag on the floor.

"If you want to turn out the light, it's on the wall by the door," she said.

"Oh no, I've been waiting patiently to make love to you and I want to be able to see every incredible glorious inch of you. I don't want darkness casting a shadow over your beauty.

He joined her on the bed and without waiting he pulled her so that she was lying flat on the bed under him. The feel of her skin against his without clothing separating them was almost his undoing.

As he lowered himself to completely cover her body with his, Michelle's arms came up to circle around his neck as her lips parted to take his kiss full on. The kiss was hard and filled with promises of a night of sensual love making. If the way he was making love to her mouth was a sign, Michelle was in for the best night of her life.

She enjoyed kissing him. His lips engulfed her very being every time he touched them to hers and tonight didn't disappoint.

Kevin groaned into her mouth as he deepened the kiss letting her know how much he wanted her.

"All day baby," he whispered in between tugs on her lips with his teeth and tongue and grinds into her body letting her know how much he wanted her.

She melted under his assault as her body rose to the occasion.

"I've been waiting all day to be here with you like this. If you didn't feel so wonderful under me I would think that this was a dream.

"It's not a dream," she said.

To prove it, she wrapped her legs around his waist just as she'd done when he first showed up, but this time there was nothing between them and she could feel his hardness as it pressed intimately into her center growing longer and thicker. She ground her body up into him as he pushed down while grinding his lower body into her. While they continued the sensual dance and kiss, she could feel his hands as they caressed every soft, curve of her body as he acquainted himself with every part of her.

Michelle writhed under him showing how ready she was for him.

Kevin read the signs clearly.

"I know baby, but I've waited all day to taste you and I don't mean just your lips. We have all night and I plan to take my time getting familiar with every part of your delicious body."

Before she could respond, Kevin kissed her one last time before moving further down her body. He kissed her chin and then her neck and her mews grew louder as he found his way to her ample breasts, first taking one nipple into his mouth and then the other, taking his time to roll the hard tips between his teeth making her body rise off the bed with every nip.

"Tasty," he said looking up into her eyes as she watched him make love to her body with his mouth.

He watched as her eyes closed shut while he traveled even further down her body still licking and kissing along the way until he found the apex of her thighs, his favorite place to be. As he slid down further so that her womanhood was looking back at him, he reached down to spread her legs wide so that his mouth could become intimately connected with her.

Michelle remembered the exact moment his tongue intimately stroked her because the feeling overwhelmed her senses. Her writhing under this caress turned to thrashing about on the bed as she sighed with every pass of his tongue. When she thought she'd be able to hold out and draw out the pleasure, his tongue went into her, diving as far as it would go and along with the pressure he then applied with his thumb, she went crashing over the edge of pleasure, no longer able to control her body's reaction to his carnal attack on it.

Even though Michelle whipped about like a crazy woman, Kevin never let up. He lapped at her like she was his last meal, making sure he got every drop. As her legs quivered, he caressed them taking in her reaction to his loving under hooded eyes. Watching her in the throes of an orgasm was too much for him to stand on the sidelines and watch. He needed to get inside of her before he exploded.

Not wasting any time, he reached for one of the condoms he'd thrown on the bed and after donning the thin layer of protection, he rose so that their bodies were even and when his tongue searched out her mouth for entry, his lower body sought entry into her body. He reached down, spreading her legs further apart and with great restraint he entered her body in short yet invasive strokes. She was tight and due to his large size, he didn't want to push forward too fast causing her any pain.

Michelle thought she had died and gone to heaven. Finally she was feeling what it was like to make love to Kevin and her world exploded with exhilaration. He made her feel full as he worked himself into her body taking care to do it gently. She knew he was big from seeing him naked, but feeling his size was a different story. He felt large and engorged and she knew he would eventually seat himself all the way in. In the meantime, she loved the feel of him going in and out of her body. She wasn't sure how more of the slowness she'd be able to take. She wanted all of him and she wanted it now.

"Don't hold back. I need you Kevin; I need all of you, please!" she heard herself begging.

"I could hurt you if we don't take it slow baby because you really are tight. I want to please you, not make this painful for you."

"It's more painful waiting than anything else. Don't be gentle with me. I need all of you right now. I want to feel every delightful inch of you."

Kevin didn't want her to want any more so following his last pull out of her body, he surged all the way in until he was in as far as he would go. He looked at her to be sure she wasn't in pain. He knew she wasn't when her legs encased his body and she ground up into him. Using that as a sign that she was okay, he began stroking into her long and hard giving them both what they needed.

"Like this baby?" he asked, never missing a stroke while adding a circular motion to his hips.

"Yes!"

That's all he needed to hear.

"Hold on baby, this ride is about to get a little bumpy."

Michelle was more than ready and as he pushed harder into her she sucked up every stroke, meeting him stroke for stroke loving the feel of his entry over and over again into her body. As he rode her she could feel a tingling that started in her toes and soon rose through her legs to land in the apex of her thighs where their bodies were joined intimately. The feeling made her nipples harden as Kevin reached up to pinch first one then the other causing the dual sensation to cause stars to form behind her eyelids.

Michelle used her inner muscles to grip him hard and the feeling sent them cresting at the same time as she did. She couldn't hold back the scream that escaped.

"Kevin, yes!" she shouted as she continued to ride the wave that slammed into her body. The stars she originally saw behind her eyes now turned into fireworks as her orgasm slammed into her again and again.

Kevin couldn't breathe. He knew he was done for the moment he felt her muscles tighten around him, gripping him for dear life. He knew he wouldn't be able to hold back anymore and the feel of her orgasm triggered his and he surged forward giving her as much as he was receiving.

"Ah, Michelle," he groaned out his release. It continued on until the cresting began subsiding. As his body calmed and he could think and speak again, he lifted off of her body and looked in her eyes.

"Incredible baby. I knew making love to you would be like this and I plan to do it all night long."

He kissed her letting her feel in his kiss his intent to follow through with his promise.

"I look forward to it," she said going into his embrace as he moved to the side of her and drew her up against him.

**

Anger stronger than anything he had ever experienced before rose up and took control of Max's every thought. His hand began pounding over and over again on his thigh. The anger was so strong, he barely felt it. Just as he had worked up the nerve to walk across the street and knock on Michelle's door, another man shows up. That new invasion on the life he was planning for him and Michelle didn't sit well. He wasn't sure what the relationship was between Michelle and the mystery man, but the man looked familiar to him. He only got a good look for a split second when the he passed below the street light and something about his demeanor seemed familiar. Familiar or not he didn't like how happy Michelle was to see him when she opened her door. Before they went inside he was able to see that she looked as beautiful as she always had to him. Thinking of her beauty and the perfect life they were going to have together tampered down his anger a bit. She was his woman and unless this guy was just a casual friend, there was going to be trouble. The man was definitely bigger than he was, but that didn't matter to him. If he had to get rid of him because he may stand in the way of him and Michelle being together, he would do that without blinking. Michelle was his and no one was going to stand in the way of that.

He'd been sitting outside of her house for hours in the car after the man showed up, wondering if he'd be leaving soon. After getting out and pacing the sidewalk in disgust that the man could be making love to his Shelly, he knew he wouldn't be able to get to her this time. There would be another day, he said to himself, walking back into the shadows of the night and getting back into his car. He knew if she were cozying up to some new guy, he had to make a move soon to get her away from him and everyone else. Soon it would only be him and her, forever.

The Dancer - 10

Michelle was excited about her planned evening. After a week of not being able to spend any time with Kevin because he was busy at work and she was busy at her studio, as well as with her Broadway performances, they were finally carving out some time for dinner and a movie. They would also get the chance to talk because Kevin wanted to talk to her about telling Casey that they were seeing each other. He knew Casey would be fine with it, but he wanted them to talk through how to approach it so that she understood that it wouldn't take time away that he spent with her when they planned Disney movie nights loaded down with pizza and other snacks. Kevin made sure he still spent quality time with Casey while also juggling work and his relationship with her.

It had been a week since they'd made love and

the relationship only got stronger after they spent the night together. She loved waking up in the morning after only an hour's worth of sleep after making love throughout the night. She woke up to kisses all over her body before Kevin made love to her one last time before he had to leave to pick up Casey to drop her off at school and then get to work on time. She was a walking zombie all day, but she knew it was all worth it. She'd give up many more nights of sleep just to make love with him again and she looked forward to when they would.

Tonight was date night though and they wanted to get out and do something together.

As they settled in for the ride to the movie theater, Michelle looked at Kevin and saw worry lines. She assumed something about work had him unnerved. She didn't know whether to pry, not wanting him to reveal anything about work that he shouldn't tell her, but she was still concerned. She had come to care a lot about him and she hurt if anything hurt him.

She'd learned a lot about him in the many conversations they'd had. He'd shared with her the story behind Casey's mother's death and how he hadn't been involved with anyone seriously since her. He felt partly responsible because he believed he didn't do all he could have done to make her feel more loved and secure. Michelle sympathized with him. She could hear the hurt and pain in his voice.

She remembers being on the phone and wishing

that she were in his presence so that she could comfort him. She was already growing more and more fond of him just from their talks.

Kevin was unlike any man she'd ever met. He was more than caring. He really wanted to protect everyone he came in contact with and to her, he was a true protector in every sense of the word. She knew that if he could have done more to keep Casey's mother from going down the path she chose, he would have. If he had known that she needed more of his time and attention, Michelle had no doubt he would have given it to her. She felt bad that he didn't get the chance to fix what was wrong in his marriage.

Once they were able to get beyond the discussion of his sad past, they were able to talk about happier times.

She was reluctant to tell him about Max and the devastating affect that relationship had on her. When he'd interviewed her, she told him only what she thought he needed to know, but it was during the conversations where they were sharing more details about themselves that she told him more about the bad parts of her relationship with Max. Kevin didn't comment, he just listened.

After hearing her stories of ups and downs with Max, he let her know that he would never do anything to hurt her or to curb her independence. It was one of the things that drew him to her and he wouldn't want to change that about her.

She was glad they were able to get that out of the way because she wanted to look towards happier times and she hoped it would consist of the two of them together.

She told him all about her family back in Virginia and how much she missed them and the fact that she hadn't told them about the attack yet, but that she planned to once the guy was caught and she could ease their minds that she would be okay.

"I've missed you this week," she said trying to break into his troubled thoughts. When he didn't respond, she knew then that he was still distracted.

"Kevin, what's wrong?"

"What?" he said turning briefly toward her before turning back to the evening traffic.

"Something is wrong and I'm concerned. You seem distant and preoccupied tonight. Do you want to forget about dinner and the movie tonight? If so I understand because I know these cases have you on edge."

Kevin should have been more careful with his thoughts when he picked her up. He didn't want her concerned with what was going on with him. He knew before the evening was over he'd have to tell her about the progress made in the case, but he didn't want it to overshadow their night together. He needed to tell her and get it out of the way.

So that he wasn't distracted while driving, he pulled over and parked. He then turned to her.

"Michelle we have a few developments in the case. For starters, we've located two of the missing dancers. They were found dead inside of cars in the river. It looks like they've both been there for a few weeks. Some divers going on a tip found them this morning and we've kept the story out of the news hoping to get some clues before the media got a hold of it. Also, another woman was attacked last night in a car not far from where we found the other two dancers in the river. She wasn't able to tell us much before losing consciousness. I'm hoping to get the chance to talk to her more soon. I'm waiting on the autopsies of the two found in the river to see what the cause of death was and whether they died before or after being in the water. The discovery weighed heavily on me today and all I could think about was seeing you, holding you and making love to you because I know that when I'm with you, you're safe. If the guy who attacked them is the same one who attacked you, the shock of what could have happened to you settled over me and I haven't been able to shake it."

Michelle could see the weight he was carrying in his eyes before he turned away from her and she didn't want that. She needed him to know she was fine.

"Kevin, look at me baby."

He turned to her with concern still on his face.

"I'm fine and whoever this guy is, I know you're going to find him soon and we can put all of this behind us. At least it appears it was some random attack and not someone out to get me. I know you've been worried about that too. Get rid of the burden of what could have happened to me. I'm fine and as soon as the other woman wakes up, she'll give you information and you'll be able to catch this guy before he hurts anyone else and finally you'll be able to put this behind you and we won't have to worry about this anymore. Why don't we forget about the dinner and movie and just go back to my house and relax. I can just as easy cook us a nice dinner."

"I wanted us to get out and do something. I love being with you no matter what we're doing, but I feel like we don't get to go out often because of my work. Let's stick to the plan of dinner and a movie and then we can relax at your house or my house later."

Michelle nodded her agreement. She liked the sound of them relaxing later and she would love to go to his house. She'd been there a few times and loved how big and soft his bed was.

"That sounds good to me. I know you wanted to talk about telling Casey about us. Do you still want to do that?" she asked.

"Of course I do and Casey is going to be excited about it. I just wanted to talk it out to be sure you were ready for it. I've been ready because I've fallen in love with you and I want her know how much you mean to me."

Michelle wasn't surprised at his declaration. Kevin wore his heart on his sleeve. She was just happy they were in this together and on the same page.

"I love you too Kevin and I'm ready whenever you are."

He leaned over and kissed her softly.

"Let's do it tomorrow when I pick her up from dance class. We could take her out to get something to eat and tell her then. How does that sound?" he asked.

She smiled loving where their relationship was going. "That sounds like a great plan to me."

Kevin smiled, feeling better than he had when they first set out. He pulled back into traffic to get to the movie on time.

Michelle was right. As soon as the woman woke up, he'd get to talk to her and hopefully she'll give them enough details to catch the guy.

**

The hour was getting late. Where could she be at this hour? She had better not still be out with the man he saw going into her house earlier. Max waited up the block until they had gotten in the man's car and drove away.

After walking away, his footsteps led him back to her street, across from her house. He needed to see her. He wanted to talk to her and apologize for attacking her. He knew that if he said he was sorry, she would forgive him and see how much they should be together.

He had their life all planned out. They would move away from everyone they knew so that no one would be able to convince her that he wasn't the man for her. They would settle down someplace, have the children he knew she wanted and they'd wonderful life. There was no way he could live his life without her.

He knew she still loved him and all she needed was a fresh start to a new life in a place where he wouldn't have to worry about other people. He loved her and no one loved as much as he did.

Now this man she was out with is another thing that could come between them and he couldn't have that. He needed to convince her to come away with him and he needed to do it soon. If she resisted, then he would leave her no choice, but to come with him whether she wanted to or not.

He checked his watch again. It was well after eleven at night. Where could she be? How dare she be out this late with another man? He had to put a stop to this before it went much further. She was his woman and this would be the last time she'd be around any other man.

**

"I had a wonderful time Kevin," Michelle said as they drove toward her house. It was a little after midnight. After the movie and dinner, they had gone to Rockefeller Plaza to sit and talk. It was a perfect night for doing just that. While they were there, Kevin received a phone call that another woman had been attacked and this time, the man was apprehended trying to get away.

Finally the menace was off the streets. The hour was late, but Kevin's captain wanted him back at work while the information was still fresh and the woman was able to tell them everything about the circumstances surrounding her attack.

"I did too and I'm sorry we have to cut our plans short of spending some relaxing time together. I know we were going to go to my house tonight and you still can. Since tomorrow is a late start day for you, you can sleep late and you'd already be in bed waiting for me whenever I'm done at the precinct."

"Kevin, you could be all night and I don't want you worrying about getting me back home in the morning. Just drop me off at my house and if you feel like it when you're done, come by. Besides, I'm closer than you and you won't have far to go to drop me off and get to the precinct. I know you're anxious to get all of the details."

Kevin had to agree her plan was better than his.

"Okay, I'll do that. I don't think it will take all night so I'll call you when I'm on my way."

They pulled up to her house and he saw no place to park.

"Don't park. I'll be fine from here and you can watch me as I go inside."

"I'll just leave the car here and walk you to the door," he said double parking in front of her door.

He kissed her before making sure she had locked the door after going inside. He then raced back to his car and sped in the direction of the precinct. They had their man in custody.

**

Max's anger boiled over when he saw the man lean down and kiss his Shelly. He knew then that she was a liar and a cheater just as he had suspected she was. He knew she was lying every time she said she wasn't seeing anyone else. She was no better than the other women he knew, the ones who were lying in a grave at the bottom of the Hudson River.

They'd met their fate and now it was time for Shelly to meet hers. He exited the car and walked toward her house. He hesitated, looking down the street to be sure the man had driven off, not to return. When he didn't see anything, he rang the bell and hid his face from the peep hole. He then realized there was no need. He could hear her taking the lock off of the door.

"Did you forget something?" Michelle said opening the door. Before she could take in that the person on the other side of the door was Max and not Kevin, he'd forced is way inside covering her screams with his hand. He shoved her backwards and shut the door behind them.

The Dancer - 11

Kevin sprinted into the precinct as soon as he parked his car. He went in search of his captain through the maze of the office full of officers working at midnight. Normally they had a scaled back over night force, but he assumed with the capture of the attacker, all hands were on deck.

"Kevin, I need to see you in my office," his captain said when he spotted him.

Kevin looked in the face of his boss and saw the seriousness. He followed him in to his office.

"What's up?" he asked, entering and taking a seat in the chair across the desk.

"For starters, our team did a great job of catching this guy. Some people heard the woman scream as she sat in a car with this guy near the pier where we found the other women submerged in those cars. They said they were out walking when they heard the commotion in the car. They ran over to help and the guy in the car bolted. The men chased him down and when they saw some cops they flagged them down while they still gave chase saying they saw him assaulting a woman. The cops gave chase as well and tackled the guy. He's in a cell now. I figured you'd want to question him."

Kevin definitely wanted to do that. He needed to put this case to rest and to also confirm the same guy had attacked Michelle, putting them both at ease that he'd been caught.

"Thanks Cap, this is all great news. How is the woman doing?"

"She's going to be fine. She's already been checked out by the hospital and is on her way here. She said she wanted to come in and give us all of the details while they were fresh."

"Great. I want to talk to her when she gets here too," Kevin said turning to leave.

"Kevin wait, there's one more thing."

Kevin waited as an emotion that looked like dread appeared on his face. His captain continued to stare at Kevin as if he were struggling with his next words.

"Spit it out Captain," Kevin said, losing patience.

"Okay here it is. This guy didn't attack Michelle."

"What? How do you know that?"

"He's already admitted to attacking the woman tonight and to the attacks on several other women, but none of those women were dancers and the night Michelle was attacked he was locked up in jail on a public nuisance charge. They kept him there from four in the afternoon until early the next morning so he couldn't have done it."

Kevin didn't like the sound of what he was hearing.

"Are you sure about all of this?" he said.

"I am and there is one more thing you need to know. The other woman who was attacked and had been unconscious is now awake. I suggest before you interview anyone else, you start with her. We already know our guy in custody attacked this woman tonight, but we need to know if he also attacked the woman in the hospital."

"Understood," Kevin replied. "Will they let me in tonight to see her at this hour? I know how protective they are of questioning patients this time of night."

"Yes. She had them call us and asked for an officer to come. Just flash your badge and you'll get through. Go do that now. The guy in custody isn't going anywhere tonight."

**

Kevin walked behind the nurse into the hospital room of the woman who was attacked and survived. Perhaps, he thought, he could finally get someplace in the investigation. It was clear that the man in custody could not have attacked Michelle and something about it still pricked the back of his mind. He had an uncomfortable feeling that he was missing something.

As he approached her bedside, she opened her eyes.

"Hello, I'm Detective Garner."

Kevin showed her his badge to put her at ease. "Is it okay if I ask you a few questions about the night you were attacked? Anything you can possibly remember would be helpful."

"Sure," she said.

Kevin watched as she struggled through the pain of the attack to sit up. He could see clear signs of the attempted strangulation around her neck. He was able to gather from the reports of the autopsy of the other women found submerged in cars in the river that they'd died from asphyxiation. He was glad those reports were on his desk when he arrived at the precinct. He had no doubt the same person who killed them had also attacked the woman in the bed.

"The man who attacked you, did you know him or had you met him prior to that night?"

"I didn't know him personally, but he came into a club where I was working. He flirted a little bit and offered me a lot of money to spend the night with him. We left the club, got in his car and he drove to a pier. I asked why we weren't going to his place, he said he was anxious and couldn't wait. He wanted a little taste right there. I knew I shouldn't have, but I went along with it because it was a lot of money."

Kevin didn't want to seem judgmental and tried to show no emotion about her reason for being with the guy.

"You know there were two other women who were found dead right off of that pier. We didn't find them until after you were attacked, but my guess is he had the same fate for you in mind."

"It terrifies me to know that I could have ended up like them. I guess I was lucky," she said.

Kevin knew she was right; luck was on her side that night.

"Can you tell me anything you can remember about what he looked like? Is there anything significant about this guy that stood out to you?"

Kevin took notes as she began describing the man who attacked her. He stopped writing when she realized one important thing about that night.

"He kept calling me Shelly."

Kevin's pulse quickened.

"What do you mean? Is that a nickname for you? I understand your name is Tammy."

"Yes, my name is Tammy and I told him several times that my name was Tammy, but he said for that night he needed me to answer to Michelle or Shelly. He said the deal was off if he couldn't call me that, so I went along with it."

That uneasy feeling Kevin had, now began to make him anxious.

"Did he say why he needed you to do that?"

"Yes, he said that was the name of his ex-girlfriend and that he loved and missed her and I resembled her."

Kevin looked closer at her and something stuck out that he didn't realize on his way to the hospital. She looked like Michelle and so did the other women who were attacked and were found dead. It wasn't an exact replica, but in darkness and at just the right angle, she looked like Michelle. That gave him an eerie feeling. He listened closely as Tammy continued.

"I figured maybe she had died and he wanted to live out some fantasy that she was still alive. He kept talking about how pretty she was and that like me she was a dancer. Once we were at the pier, as I was going down on him, he became angry, yelling at me, saying I was going to get what I deserved for leaving him and cheating on him and then I felt his hands tighten around my neck. He kept saying 'Shelly, it's your time to die' and he started choking me. I started fighting back and when I realized I was about to die, I fought harder and I started ramming him with my head and after one good jam and he released my neck and buckled over. I tried to scramble away to get out of the car and he started beating me."

"You were brave Tammy. How were you able to get out of the car?"

"We started to struggle and once I was able to really get up on the seat, I used my feet to push him away and with my hands I struggled with the door handle and when it opened I fell out. I wasn't sure how far I'd get if I ran because I could barely breathe and my eye was swollen so bad from him hitting me that I couldn't see out of it. Just then some men started screaming, asking what was going on and that's the last thing I remember. I think that's when I passed out."

Kevin knew what happened then. The men who heard and saw the struggle came over to help and the man in the car with Tammy ran off.

"Oh, one more thing," she said, getting his attention.

"What's that?" he asked curiously.

"Right before I passed out he said 'you got away this time Shelly, but I'm coming for you and you won't get away again'. His voice sounded crazed."

Kevin now knew why he had the uncomfortable feeling. Something was telling him he knew who the guy was, but he needed proof.

"Tammy, if I can have a little more of your time, I'm going to get someone to send me a picture I have at the station and I want you to see if you recognize him."

"Sure, if it will help catch this creep because whoever this Shelly person is, I have a feeling she wasn't dead as I thought. I think she's still alive and just left him and if so, she may be next."

Those were Kevin's thoughts exactly. He shook nervously as he pulled out his cell phone to call the station. He had a feeling Tammy was right and in the back of his mind, he knew who Shelly was. He felt a little relief knowing she was safe at home behind locked doors with her alarm on.

His captain answered on the first ring.

"Captain, I need a quick favor. In my office there's the case folder for Michelle Hitchens. Inside is a picture of her ex-boyfriend that she provided us with when we were looking into anyone who may have had something against her. Take a picture of his picture and send it to my phone."

"I'm on it," his captain replied.

Kevin waited and within a few minutes he had his picture. He showed it to Tammy.

"Take your time and look at this guy and tell me if he looks anything like the guy who attacked you."

Kevin watched as fear like none he'd ever seen before crossed Tammy's face.

"Yes, that's him," she shouted.

"You're sure?"

"Yes, I'm positive. That's definitely the man."

Kevin's heart began to beat a million miles a minute. He thought back to his initial assumption after Michelle's attack when he thought he'd heard her attacker say her name. He'd been correct and the fact that he didn't stick with his initial thought unnerved him. He wasted no time in what he knew he had to do.

"Thank you Tammy. There will be an officer outside your room just for added protection. You've just helped me solve this case. I'm glad you're going to be okay and I'm going to catch this guy so that he doesn't hurt anyone else."

Kevin turned and jetted out of the room as fast as he could without causing alarm with hospital staff. As he rushed to his car, he called his captain using his work cell and with his other cell he dialed Michelle at home. He knew she should be there because he'd dropped her off a few hours ago when he was summoned to the precinct.

"Captain, the picture you sent me is the guy we're looking for. The woman in the hospital recognized him without any doubt. He's also the man that attacked Michelle. It's her ex-boyfriend, Max. I told you how I thought I heard the guy say something the night of her attack before he ran off. I heard him call her by name and I let that go when I was convinced I could have been hearing things since it could have been any number of people who were on the street that night talking. Now I know it's fact and if I'm correct, Michelle is in danger and I need to get to her to be sure she is safe."

Kevin was alarmed that Michelle's phone kept ringing and then going to voicemail. Even if she'd fallen asleep already, she would always answer her phone. He needed to get to her.

"Kevin, I'll get some guys and meet you there."

His captain hung up and Kevin jumped in his car, turned on his flashers and headed to Michelle's house.

He prayed all the way there hoping she was

okay.

**

"Max, what are you doing? You know sooner or later someone is going to be looking for me," Michelle said.

She watched as Max continued packing a bag with clothes from her closet as if he were helping her pack for a vacation. She was sitting on the floor at the foot of her bed not moving. She could tell that Max was borderline psychotic and she didn't know what he would do if she tried to get away. She tried talking to him which always helped in the past.

"You mean your cop boyfriend? I'm not worried about him. Once we're out of New York, we won't have to worry about him or anyone else. It didn't dawn on me until I saw him leave tonight that he's the same cop who was on the street the night I tried to grab you. I bet you were screwing him the whole time we were involved. Well not anymore so I hope you said goodbye earlier. That was your last time seeing him."

Michelle thought back to Kevin's initial thought that he'd heard her attacker say her name.

"It was you that night who tried to drag me in an alley. You were the attacker. What were you thinking doing that Max? What are you thinking now? This is crazy. I'm not going anywhere with you."

"Of course you are. You and I are getting out of

New York and we're going to live in a place where no one can find us and disturb our lives. We've been apart too long. We are meant to be together Shelly and I'm taking you some place where you won't be tempted to cheat on me with other men."

"Max, I've never cheated on you with other men and we are not a couple now. What we had ended a long time ago and I've moved on just like you should have."

Apparently that angered him as he came up to her sneering.

"I don't have to move on because you belong to me. You're lucky I've decided to give you another chance and not choke the life out of you like I did those other women who were substitutes for you. Because of the sacrifice they made, you're able to live so you should be thanking me at this point. Shut up, let me finish what I'm doing and we'll get going."

Michelle trembled when a menacing look crossed Max's face.

"Max, what are you saying?"

Realization set in and Michelle started putting all the pieces together.

"You tried to grab me that night on the street all because of your obsession with controlling me."

More realization came over her.

"What else have you don't Max?"

Max didn't miss a beat in responding.

"Lucky for you I was unsuccessful that night

because if I had been successful, we wouldn't be having this conversation right now; you'd be dead."

"Kevin was right when he said he heard you say my name after the attack. I brushed it off and told him it couldn't have been you. What happened to you? Why are you doing this?"

"I'm doing this because I love you and you love me."

"Max, what else have you done?"

She wasn't sure she wanted to know, but she needed to buy as much time as she could while she figured out what to do.

When he didn't answer, but continued moving around her room, she asked again.

"Max, if I'm going to go with you and build this life you're talking about, you're going to have to tell me everything."

He stopped when she said that and she figured in his mind, all he heard was her readiness to build a life with him.

"Well I had to take my aggression about not having you in my life anymore out on a few other women and it's all your fault. My anger got the best of me and I killed them and dumped their bodies in the river."

Michelle knew he was referring to the women Kevin told her had been found in the river immersed in cars, strangled.

"Now that you're going to live your life out with me, I don't think anyone else needs to die, but don't test me Michelle. I promise you will not like the outcome. There is more room at the bottom of the river for you too, now let's go."

Michelle stumbled as Max grabbed her up off of the floor and headed back down the stairs to the door.

"Max don't do this," she pleaded.

"Shut up Michelle and stop making me angry. You don't want to see the angry me," he demanded, roughly pulling her down the stairs.

They entered her garage and he placed her in her car before going around to the driver's side. She watched as he put her keys in the ignition, opened the garage door and backed out. She had to figure out a way to get away from him. Even though he spoke of them having this great life together, she had a feeling her life was in danger. She was glad she thought to grab her cell phone as they passed it on the way to the car.

Daylight was coming up and she knew soon Kevin would show up and realize something was out of order. She knew the ringing house phone that rang constantly was him and she knew he'd be concerned and come to check on why she wasn't answering. She was glad her cell phone was on vibrate so that Max couldn't hear it ringing.

**

Something was definitely wrong. As Kevin pulled up to Michelle's house and saw her wide open garage with her car missing, he knew Michelle wouldn't leave her garage door up after pulling out. He also knew she wouldn't leave out after midnight and if there had been an emergency, she would have called him since she knew he'd be stopping by after his business at the precinct.

He left his car in the middle of the street and walked into the garage, noticing immediately that the door that led into her house was not only unlocked, but it was left wide open.

As he entered he could hear other sirens blaring as back-up rushed toward the house. He entered with caution, drawing his weapon as he eased the door open, listening for any sound. Not hearing any he moved further into the house as he was then joined by other members of his team.

They searched and found no sign of Michelle. Kevin found her purse, the lights were left on and when he got to her bedroom, things were strewn all over as his level of worry went sky high.

"He has her," he said when he was joined by his captain.

"You're probably right and we have no idea how much of a head start he has on us. We've put out a 'be on the lookout' for them and Michelle's car."

Kevin heard him, but he wasn't listening. Knowing a BOLO was out was fine, but he needed to find her. All he could think about was the fate of the other women Max had encountered and he needed to find Michelle before something horrible happened to her as well.

He loved her and he didn't want anything to happen to her. He remembered the feelings he felt when he lost his wife and he didn't want to suffer through that kind of loss again. He couldn't protect his wife like he knew he should have, but he wasn't going to stand by and let the same fate befall Michelle. He had to do something.

"Captain, I'm hitting the streets. I need to find Michelle. There's no telling what this psycho would be doing to her and I need to get to her."

"Kevin, I understand, but take a few of the guys with you and stay in touch. I'm going back to the precinct to see what we can turn up and I'll let you know what we find out."

Kevin nodded and headed for the door when his cell phone rang. It was Michelle's number.

"Captain, it's Michelle."

Kevin's heart began beating fast as he answered.

"Michelle, are you alright?" he asked trying to hold some composure. The hairs on his skin stood up when she didn't respond.

"Michelle?"

Again he got no response. He heard his captain in the background yelling to someone to call the precinct and get a location on a tower nearest to where Michelle was calling from.

"Get that location over my car radio," Kevin said sprinting to his car with every member of his team running behind him to their cars.

He continued calling her name and when he still

received no response, he listened. He could hear a man and a woman talking and recognized Michelle's voice.

"Michelle? Can you hear me? Are you okay?" he asked.

When she didn't respond he pulled into traffic and continued to listen. Something was going on, on the other side of the phone. It's a good thing he decided to calm down and listen in. Michelle was trying to send him a message about where they were.

He could hear her saying things to Max about sights they were passing. It was a clue and Kevin didn't waste any time. He threw his siren on and headed in the direction of the markers he recognized from her clues. To be safe, he placed his phone on mute so that noise from his end of the phone couldn't be heard.

Just as his car radio gave him information on the location of where Michelle's cell phone was pinging he knew he was only a few blocks away. He didn't want Max to see or hear them coming so he put out a call for all cars to turn their sirens off because they were going to catch up to them on silent. He turned his off and drove a little faster. Luckily his team were all in unmarked cars so he was sure they wouldn't spook Max until they were up on him.

Kevin drove faster, weaving in and out of traffic and then he saw them. They weren't in a hurry and had not spotted him or his team yet.

He radioed everyone again telling them to lay back some while he tried to get closer to assess what was happening in the car. He got as close to them as he could trying to get Michelle's attention and then he gathered Max noticed him in the rearview mirror. Kevin saw him turn and look directly at him. He knew from the look on his face that Max knew who he was.

Where he thought he was going to be the element of surprise, he was surprised himself at being recognized.

"Your boyfriend is following us."

Michelle turned and saw Kevin in the car following them. Her idea to dial his number so that he could hear her without Max realizing it worked. She wasn't sure how things were going to turn out, but at least she knew Kevin knew she was in danger.

"Just pull over Max and let me out. Don't make this worse."

"Shut up Shelly," Max said as he floored her Honda.

Kevin turned his siren on and pursued them. He didn't know what was happening in the car, but he needed to get Michelle away from him. Various options began running through his mind since they were heading into some pretty heavy traffic.

Just as Max had to slow down in order to get around some cars that had stopped upon hearing the siren on Kevin's car, he watched with horror as the door on Michelle's side of the car opened and she fell from the car and rolled over several times. Thankfully they were going slow enough that no other car on the street had hit her.

He wanted to continue on after Max, but decided to stop for Michelle instead. When he did, he signaled to the other officers who were also a part of the chase to continue on after Max. His car had barely come to a stop when he jumped out and ran to make sure Michelle was okay.

"Baby, say something," he said when he reached her and rolled her over slowly making sure he didn't injure her more if she was hurt. He noticed her eyes were still closed and she wasn't moving. "Michelle, can you hear me baby? Please wake up?" he said, throatily.

Michelle opened her eyes at the sound of the love of her life. It took her a few moments to take in her surroundings and remember what was going on. When she tried to move, she winced in pain. She had leaped out of a moving car to get away from Max. It was a spur of the moment decision to jump out of the car, but now that she was looking up into the eyes of the man she loved, she knew everything was going to be okay.

"Michelle can you hear me?"

She was groggy, but alert enough to respond, easing his worry.

"I'm fine though the aches and pains all over my body could tell a different story."

Kevin sighed with relief hearing the sweet sound of her voice. It didn't mean she wasn't badly injured but for now, at least she was awake.

"What were you thinking jumping from a moving car? You could have been killed?"

"I know, but if I hadn't he was probably going to kill me and I needed to get away and that was the only thing I could think of. Once I knew you were behind us, I knew you'd be here to help me."

She tried to sit up and look around, but when she tried, her head started to spin so she laid back down on the grass.

"Max is going to get away. He killed those women Kevin; women who reminded him of me."

Michelle was again terrified, even while lying in Kevin's arms safe. She was devastated when Max told her of his attempts to remove thoughts and images of her from his mind by taking his hatred for her out on other women. She felt sorry for the women and for the families of those women who were now suffering because of her relationship with Max. She began to cry and Kevin pulled her a little tighter in his embrace to comfort her. His loving arms felt good, but they didn't erase the fact that because of her women were dead.

"Babe, please don't worry about that right now. An ambulance is on the way and I need to get you to the hospital to see if you have any injuries that I can't see. Lay still until they get here.

The Dancer
Epilogue

"What will happen to Max?"

Kevin was just settling in for the night in bed next to Michelle and the last thing he wanted to talk about was a lunatic who had kidnapped her and probably would have killed her. He was happy he'd reached them when he did.

"Michelle, baby, I know you can't seem to let this go, but I want you too. Max needs help and he's going to get the help he needs. At least the families of those women now have closure. I want you to have some closure as well."

Michelle snuggled up closer to Kevin loving the comfort of being safe in his arms. She wanted to remove all thoughts of Max to enjoy spending the night at Kevin's house wrapped up in his loving arms.

Her family had come to town and were staying at her house.

After Max had been caught and arrested and she was given the all clear from the hospital, she'd come back home and made the call she had been dreading. Within a few hours, her entire family had come to New York to check on her to be sure she really was okay. Although she tried to tell them she was perfectly fine, they needed to see for themselves.

The trip had actually turned out to be a good one because her family got to meet Kevin and Casey and her parents and sisters loved him. He was easily able to convince her family that she was fine, that Max was never going to hurt her or any other woman ever again and that he loved her and would make it his job to always protect her. She was glad because Kevin and her father, having a lot in common, got along like they'd known each other a lifetime.

After having dinner with her family, she decided to spend the night with Kevin and Casey because she'd gotten comfortable being close to them and she didn't want to spend the night away from him.

"I know I need to move on from all of the drama, but it's hard to think that women have died because of my relationship with Max and that sickens me."

"You can't be responsible for what Max did. I don't expect you to forget it, but I'm hoping you now see that it's over and you can move on with your life."

"I want that too. Is Casey asleep already?"

"Yes, I told her you were spending the night and in the morning I was going to make us some really fluffy pancakes, which happened to be her favorite."

"Wow, you cook too? I'll have to keep you around forever now," she said, reaching up to capture his lips in a soft kiss.

"I like the sound of that. I never want to let you go. When I think that I could have lost you, I wasn't sure I would have survived. Now that I know it's over and I have you here in my arms where you should always be, I can't wait to see where our relationship takes us. I never thought I'd love like this ever again. I love you baby," he said, rolling Michelle so that she was under him. Before she could say another word, their lips met in an intoxicating kiss at the same time as she felt her night shirt being removed from her body.

"I love you too. Love me baby," she said as she opened her heart a little more to him as well as her body. She removed all thoughts from her mind of nothing but how Kevin was making her feel.

"I plan to do that all night long," he said.

Before she could reply, she opened her legs wider to accept his loving as he entered her body slowly, taking his time to love her at a pace that gave them time to appreciate the love that flowed between them.

As Kevin began his slow, penetrating grind into

her body, she wrapped her legs around his waist, crossing them above his hips accepting every stroke in and out of her body. She joined in the lovemaking, matching his strokes adding in upward thrusts of her own.

Michelle relaxed into the kiss that was sending her higher and higher knowing that their love was as everlasting as the passion that filled the room.

"I want to be like this with you forever," she whispered as the pace quickened and her body burned with desire to reach that precipice with him.

"I love you baby," Kevin said as he felt her shatter under him and without delay he leaped off the cliff with her, rejoining their lips again to drown out the sounds of the quaking his body was experiencing."

When Michelle could breathe again and with her body satiated from his intense love for her, as exhaustion was surely calling her, she held on to him a little tighter wanting to stay intimately connected to him as he stayed sheathed within her body, she whispered words of love over and over again until sleep called them both.

Next from Author Cheryl Barton

The next installment of the Amorous Occupations series, *The Electrician*.

The party invitation said everyone had to wear a masquerade mask the entire night, a New Orleans tradition.   Dara Marshall couldn't resist the opportunity to spend an uninhibited night of passion with National Football Association coach Nelson Riley, the guest of honor, knowing that her identity was hidden by her mask.

Dara's world turns upside down when she discovers the gorgeous coach is the newest client of her father's business and after she's sent on the job to re-wire his condo, she does everything in her power to not give away her secret, but even behind her baggy overalls Nelson could never forget the sexy temptress he'd spent an unforgettable night with.

Available November 2014

Coming November 2014, *Heartthrob*

Cade Walker is a drop-dead gorgeous actor, the #1 box-office draw and recently named the sexiest man of the year. He's living life at the top with a bevy of beauties at his beck and call, thinking his life was perfect because of fame, fortune and five-star friends. Life changed the day he met struggling stylist, Callie Hurston, and he realized what his life was missing was unconditional love.

**

Coming December 2014, Twelve *Bachelors for Sale*

Take a look as "Twelve Bachelors for Sale" delves into the hot, sexy, stimulating, racy, erotic, sensual stories of the adventures of twelve bachelors who participated in the bachelor auction in "Bachelor Not For Sale," the first novel from Author Cheryl Barton.

Not even an ice challenge will be able to cool you down after reading about these men who are too hot to be forgotten.

All novels available on the Author's website at www.cherylbarton.net

Amorous Occupations, Book 1 - *THE ARTIST*

Zora Michaels, a local Boston artist spends all of her time working and focused on her next achievement. The war in Iraq took the life of the one man who loved her and her bohemian, artsy lifestyle. She no longer wants love. She only wants to paint.

Micah Prentiss had the perfect life, a beautiful wife, a baby about to come into the world, when that world changed with her sudden passing during child-birth. The only love he ever wanted to experience again was the love he had for his child until the passion he found in a painting reminded him of what true love is all about.

After heartache, can Zora and Micah find love again?

~~

Amorous Occupations, Book 2 – *THE BOOKKEEPER*

FBI agent Karen Jacobs is finally getting her first undercover assignment as a bookkeeper, an easy transition for her with her background in finance.

Business owner Thomas Atwater couldn't believe his eyes when he saw the love of his life walk into the restaurant where he was having lunch. Seeing her sparked feelings he thought had died long ago when she walked out on him.

Karen, discovering the object of the investigation is Thomas, the one and only man she ever truly loved, has to find a way to do her job while fighting feelings for him that she thought she had buried years ago.

Amorous Occupations Book 3 – *THE CHEF*

Master Chef Charles Watts missed out on an opportunity to purchase the building next door enabling him to expand his restaurant. His one obstacle now is that he is falling for his gorgeous neighbor while deciding what's more important to him; his sexy nights with her or his need to secure her building.

Master Baker Jenna Taylor took over the bakery her father had spent years building and then finds herself not immune to the charms of her sexy neighbor. Can she trust that his interest in her is genuine or does he have an ulterior motive?

Jenna and Charles find that the fire that's blazing is not just in their kitchens, but in the steamy nights they spend together.

OTHER BOOKS BY CHERYL BARTON:

BACHELOR SERIES:
    Bachelor Not For Sale
    A Designed Affair
    A Perfect Combination

AMOROUS OCCUPATIONS SERIES:
    The Artist
    The Bookkeeper
    The Chef

NON-SERIES TITLES:
Holly for Christmas
Second Chances: Three Valentine Novellas
Down, But Not Out: Breaking Chains

To contact and connect with Cheryl Barton:

Website: http://www.cherylbarton.net
Facebook: Author Cheryl Barton
Twitter: @mscbarton
Instagram: @authorcherylbarton

Get all novels at www.cherylbarton.net